HOUSE OF

CW01666877

PRESENTS:

RED SONYA™

OF ROGATINO

THE SHADOW OF TANAGHAARA

JAMES L. RICHARDSON

Red SonYa™ of Rogatino
The Shadow of Tanaghaara

Published by House of Crom
An Imprint of Public Domain Super Heroes
Prescott, Ontario, Canada
www.PublicDomainSuperHeroes.com

ISBN: 978-0-9784920-2-1

Cover design by James Richardson
Interior layout by James Richardson
Edited by Zara Collins

Printed in the United States of America

First Edition

HOUSE OF CROM

HOUSE OF DREAD PRESENTS:

RED SONYA™ OF ROGATINO

THE SHADOW OF TANAGHAARA

By James L. Richardson

House of Crom:
An Imprint of Public Domain Super Heroes
Prescott, Ontario, Canada

Author's Note

This story features the public domain character Red Sonya of Rogatino. If you're familiar with her original adventure from 1934, you may notice differences in personality, history, or world-building.

That's intentional.

Every book in the Public Domain Super Heroes Universe—no matter which House it falls under—is part of a larger, interconnected setting. To make that universe work, some reinterpretation of characters or their circumstances is not only allowed, but necessary.

These updates are made with genuine respect for the originals and the fans who love them. My goal isn't to overwrite their history, but to build something new from the foundations they left us.

I hope you enjoy reading these new tales as much as I enjoy crafting them.

- James Richardson
November 2025

PROLOGUE

Boot Sequence Initiate –

Impact Detected. No Activation order detected. Hold full power initiate.

Power Drain Detected – Deploy Molecular Energy Mesh.

No Tanaghaara Life Signs In Range – Priority: Power Maintenance.

Camouflage Mode – Hibernate Nano-Mech/Root Devices.

Local Organic Forms Detected: Incompatible Hosting.

Minimal Energy Draw/Solar/Organic Tap. Store All Non-Essential power.

Deploy Minimal Energy Draw To Tanaghaara Neuro Beacon.

CHAPTER 01

Knives, fists and several tankards flew past and over Sonya's head as she took the first pull of her ale. The dingy little tavern at the edge of civilization had erupted into chaos in such short order that even an experienced mercenary like Red Sonya of Rogatino had only barely enough time to duck out of the way before the first missiles slammed into wall, table and skull.

A growl grew in her chest as she slammed her tankard down on the splintered and scraped tabletop. "Idiots," she muttered. Her journey had been long, the weather uncooperative and her sore bottom and weary head had her in a foul temper even before the brawl began. She had no interest in the cause nor care for the sides in the meaningless contest, only a burning desire to make the participants pay for ruining her meal.

Wrestling her temper to heel, she assessed the combatants. The dispute was likely a local issue over missing livestock or the honour of one side's sister or daughter, but it appeared that the sides were evenly matched, with three to a side. The tavern keeper had pulled a large stick from the wood bin and was wading into one side in an attempt to club the men out of their desire to destroy his furniture and fixtures. While he was overmatched and outnumbered, he swung his makeshift weapon gamely, so Sonya turned her attention to the men on the other side of the conflict.

Two younger men were slight and under muscled compared to their opponents, but the older man, who led their efforts more than made up for the lack. A mountain of muscle hidden beneath a generous layer of fat and hair, the man's fierce demeanour gave Sonya the impression that he was both the leader and the wronged party in the dispute. She could not possibly have cared less. These idiots had already passed through the normal fists and feet of a tavern brawl and drawn knives and even a rusty sword that hadn't seen a whetstone in Sonya's lifetime.

Enough.

She shoved her rough bench back, tripping one of the slighter young men as he hurled himself across the room. He was out of the fight in an instant, a loud snap telling her he'd broken at least one bone in his ankle as he tumbled. His cry of pain was both excruciating and embarrassingly girlish.

The full tankard of ale sailed unerringly into the face of the other young man. It didn't do much damage but it caught the attention of the larger man who was lumbering across the room, three feet of rusty steel in his meaty fist. He wheeled on Sonya in fury as his companions were suddenly taken from his flanks.

"Bitch!" he snarled, raising the sword clumsily over his head. No longer a brawl, this was now a life and death struggle. A feral grin split Sonya's features as she spun to meet the threat. By size and sex, she was no match for the massive power of the man who bore down on her. By skill and experience, he stood no chance, whatever. He was dead already but didn't know it.

There wasn't enough room to swing steel in the small tavern room. The overhand strike her assailant intended might have been a threat to her in an open field, but she saw that it would foul on the low overhead beam long before it reached her skull. She whipped out a smaller, nimbler blade from the top of her tall boot and let it fly before the swing had reached its zenith. As the man's long, rusty blade caught in the rafter above his head, the point of Sonya's dagger thunked home in his throat. The sword incongruously hung above him, solidly jammed in the old oak beam, his grip on it slack as he fell face first into the dirty straw that covered the tavern floor.

"Da!" cried the man who had taken Sonya's tankard to the face. Artlessly, he leapt at Sonya, pulling a dagger of his own from his belt. She caught his wrist and with a twist, let his momentum power the throw that took him face-first into her table. Another dagger spun up into her offhand from the other boot top, and she drove it mercilessly into the flesh of his wrist between the two large bones and buried the point deeply into the tabletop.

Through broken teeth, he let loose a cry that burbled with his blood and spit, but he too was out of the fight.

Across the room, the tavern keeper had lost his battle with the other three, beaten to the floor and disarmed. The three men looked up from their efforts, surprised that their true foes hadn't set upon them from behind. They gaped at the tall redheaded woman who stood over two disabled opponents and a corpse. She wasn't even breathing heavily.

With a deadly deliberate motion, she drew her own cutlass from its scabbard and plucked a pistol from her belt with her offhand.

"Long and long have I ridden, dogs," she said quietly. "I would have my meat and mead replaced, now that your stupid brawl is quits." She pointed with her blade at the groaning innkeeper as he rolled to his knees. "Let him up, pay him what is owed and take your leave," she instructed quietly.

Reaching over she laid her pistol on the table and yanked her dagger from the wrist of the man she had pinned to the table. She wiped the blade on his dirty tunic and slid it back into her boot top. She yanked his whimpering head up by his greasy hair and shoved him at the man on the floor who stared stupidly at his mangled ankle. "Take your man and that," she pointed at the corpse in the straw, "and be glad I leave you your life."

As the three men edged past where she stood, she stopped them with the point of her sword and made it clear what she expected. They tipped her bench back to rights and two of them assisted their former foes to drag the big man's corpse from the tavern. She sheathed her cutlass and tucked her pistol back into its accustomed place in the small of her back before swinging one of her long, shapely legs over the bench and settling gratefully back onto the uncomfortable plank seat.

Before long, a fresh tankard of ale and a steaming plate of meat and vegetables slid onto the rough table, the tavern keeper's wife gabbling her thanks as she served. Sonya hardly heard her, her head buzzing with the aftermath of the unexpected combat. She ate mechanically and paid for a room with a solid door and a straw pallet. Sleep took her the instant she lay down.

She would have slept long into the day but for the pounding of angry fists on her barred door at dawn.

CHAPTER 02

The pounding at the door was courtesy of two over-muscled guardsmen, sword hands twitching as they delivered their ultimatum. Sonya scrubbed sleep from her eyes and left them little option but to wait as she slammed the rickety door in their faces while she arranged her private ablutions. When she finally emerged, the two summarily relieved her of her saber and pistols before marching her down the creaking stairs, past the few patrons in the common room. She tossed coins on the sideboard and called to the innkeeper to keep her belongings and her mount safe until her return.

The silver vanished quickly enough but the skeptical look the man's wife shot her as she passed gave Sonya reason to think that her return was by no means assured. A short cart ride delivered her to the gate of a home that in other locales might have been deemed modest, but here in the wild, disputed territory between four warring kingdoms could be termed grand. A well tended garden surrounded tidy walls punctured by windows of luridly coloured glass, all beneath a massive slate roof. To Sonya's eye, the effect was similar to a small cat arching its back and lifting its thin fur in hopes of intimidating the wolf that hunted it.

Sonya did not know to which kingdom this fiefdom owed allegiance. From what she knew of the area, the likelihood was that such loyalty was ephemeral at best, largely based on which kingdom's army was nearest to hand. That the mansion stood relatively intact at the geographic centre of a decades-long war between four aggressive and implacable neighbours was a testament to more than good fortune. If not for the rudeness of the summons, she might have found herself admiring the canniness at play.

As she had not had so much as her morning tankard of the thin local ale, admiration was not running through her as the two stocky guardsmen shoved her toward the ornately carved main door. She saw motion behind the frosted glass of one of the windows on the second floor and imagined that the observer had watched her progress across the gravel drive that led to the house from the gate where she and her two escorts had left their cart and its ponies. Wouldn't want horse shit fouling the well-tended gravel or gaily flowering decorative fauna, she reckoned.

As expected, the men escorted her up the grand staircase that dominated the entrance hall. Above all hung a massive coat of arms with two large birds of prey supporting a shield bisected, one half dominated by a bloody sword, the other, incongruously sporting what appeared to be a beehive. Ivan, a grim but stalwart comrade from her early mercenary days would have been able to explain what each symbol, colour and position on the shield and surrounding decoration represented. The pointlessness of such fripperies had her rolling her eyes as she pounded up the stairs, even without Ivan's overenthusiastic commentary on the arcane rules and practices of heraldry.

The two guards brought her before a man of middle age, his tight cropped dark brown hair surrendering to iron gray at the temples. His sharp eyes glittered, the diffuse light filtering through the stained glass windows turning his green eyes an almost golden shade as he ran his gaze from Sonya's head to the tops of her high boots. She noted that the scrutiny didn't linger overlong on her generously curved chest and immediately moved her estimation of the man upward, if only slightly. Most men and nearly every nobleman she had ever encountered tended to spend an uncomfortably long moment assessing what strained the laces of her tunic. While she could enjoy the attention and even turn it to her advantage, any man who eschewed the view or, better still, waited for permission to enjoy it was a man she noted.

Such men usually made for stout and stalwart comrades. Or formidable enemies.

Without invitation, Sonya strode up to the massive desk the man sat behind and slipped gracefully into the nearest chair on her side of it. The two guards had to quickstep to catch up. When they reached the desk, they laid her confiscated weaponry upon its gleaming surface and stepped back to stand one to either side of her chair. She ignored them completely.

For his part, the Duke simply stabbed at a rolled up slice of mutton on a plate that sat to one side of his great desk and swiped it through a bowl of white sauce before maneuvering it to his lips with the point of his dagger. He continued to watch Sonya as he chewed slowly. The man certainly enjoyed his theater.

Sonya's stomach growled loudly, reminding her that she had yet to break her fast this day. The Duke's eyebrow arched at the sound and he gallantly gestured at the tray of sliced meat in a hospitable gesture. Hardly had he made the offer than the point of Sonya's was spearing the nearest slice. She ignored the sauce and took a dainty bite of the viand from the tip of her poignard.

The Duke looked at the weapon she had drawn from the top of her high boot in surprise and then glared at the nearest guard. Sonya chewed enthusiastically and pretended not to notice the silent exchange.

Message delivered.

After a moment, the Duke waved the two guards away. They reluctantly obeyed, leaving Sonya alone with the man and his tray of delicious dainties. Without waiting for further permission, she stabbed another slice, this time sampling the tangy white sauce on one end of the tidy roll.

The Duke's eyes narrowed, but he ignored her effrontery and instead took another of the rolled slices for himself. Unlike her tidy effort, a dollop of the white sauce splattered onto the desk from his selection as he brought it to his lips. He wiped the spill up with a handkerchief he drew from his sleeve and then dabbed his lips with it before folding it neatly and setting it on the furthest corner of his desk. Doubtless some servant would ensure it was laundered and returned to him before the morning was out.

"You killed one of my serfs," said the Duke, making it obvious that he wanted her to offer her name by the way he ended the statement with an unspoken question.

"Sonya of Rogatino, my Lord," she offered. "Your serf was swinging a sword at my head at the time," she added.

"Clumsily and drunkenly, no doubt," said the Duke, not bothering to disguise his contempt for the man.

"Clumsily for a certainty. I had little time to assess his capacity for drink."

The Duke again leveled his gaze at her and folded his hands on the top of his desk before continuing. "He was a man twice your size and well acquainted with violence, yet you prevailed."

"He was a fool with a rusted blade who tried an overhand swing beneath a low ceiling," she retorted.

"So, you were in no danger from his rusted blade then?" asked the Duke with an arched brow.

"I am a lone woman," she said with a sigh. "If a man twice my size offers me violence, I do not have the luxury of giving him a second swing."

A barked laugh was his response. Without a word, he lifted a small brass bell from the desk and rang it sharply. A moment later, a young man wearing a greatcoat stumbled into the room, bowing to the Duke awkwardly as he skidded to a halt. On his shoulder, a massive hunting hawk sat on a large leather epaulet, its claws dug in fiercely enough to puncture the hide, exposing the felt padding beneath.

"This," began the Duke, gesturing at the young man, "is Aldebrand, Lord of Varn, my youngest son." From the slight puckering of his expression as he made the introduction, Sonya could see that the youngest son was certainly not the favourite. "He is in need of your..services."

Sonya looked the boy up and down. He was well formed, though the greatcoat made any assessment beyond his height and facial features a guess. He stood tall and was generally handsome, but Sonya was no harlot. "My 'services' are not on offer, my Lord," she explained with a growl.

The Lord of Varn gaped at Sonya, likely never having heard anyone gainsay his father. At least not to his face.

For his part, the Duke looked briefly puzzled and then barked another laugh. "You misunderstand Red Sonya of Rogatino. It is not your scarlet-tressed charms my son requires. I fear those beyond his ability to grapple with," he said with genuine concern. "What I require is the service of the woman who casually slides a blade past the body search of my house guards and slays my most troublesome serf with a single, casual toss of that blade."

"Ah," said Sonya. The honey had been spooned; she waited for the blade it coated.

"I have arranged a betrothal to my dear cousin's daughter and Aldebrand must travel to pledge his troth to the dear child in his person. A glance at the young man told her he was none too pleased with this arrangement, but neither had he the courage to object to it. "It is an arduous journey through the passes and winter is closing in. He requires an escort and I believe you to be a suitable escort."

"And what will be my compensation for this labour, my Lord?" asked Sonya, already knowing the terms.

"When you reach the far side of the passes and deliver my son to my cousin's care, you may continue on to wherever your mount will take you. Though I recommend not retracing your steps," said the Duke with a pointed look.

"And should I refuse this task?" she asked.

"The penalty for the killing of a serf is indentured servitude to the value of his life's estimated worth. In this case, some eight or nine years will clear your debt, I should think."

"Ah," said Sonya, feeling the honeyed blade slide home.

"It is the best bargain you'll make of this business and I would add supplies and an additional horse to the ledger as you rid me of a particularly loathsome tenant. I can offer another four men, and mounts, and of course, my son's carriage and team will be in your charge."

"And you would have me lead this expedition and take the young Lord's life into my care?" she asked. She'd been given orders by kings and cowards alike, but this was the first time she'd been offered command wrapped in a chain. It was rare for a leadership to be handed to her thus. Usually she had to wait for the men placed above her to die or flee before she found herself giving the orders rather than accepting them.

"I fear Aldebrand," said the Duke, ignoring the lad's presence, "has little experience of the fairer sex and I would have him in your company to acclimatize him before he must acquit himself in conversation with she who will be his betrothed."

It was Sonya's turn to bark a laugh.

"I shall see the boy across the passes," she surrendered with a chuckle. "Four men, two mounts a piece, your best maps, supplies for a journey of twice the distance, and enough silver at the end of it all to see me sleeping on straw-stuffed pallets for a fortnight once he has arrived hale and 'acclimatized,'" she added.

The Duke tapped his fingers on the desk, looked from the lad to Sonya and back again. "Bargain struck," he said with finality. Aldebrand flushed bright pink as his father added, "And if you can teach him to converse on a subject other than his damned bird before you arrive, I shall double the silver."

Dukes did not part with coin more than they ever had to, so she put any hope for the extra silver from her mind. Judging by the loving way the boy stroked the hawk's silky feathers, she could see there was little hope of fattening her purse in that quarter.

CHAPTER 03

As she had expected, the lad was entirely obsessed. Sonya could find no sense in it, but there it was. The boy's mind traveled in a cart track with no crossroads. In her experience, men of his age generally fell into one of two types: obsessed with women or battle. This boy had found a third path and focused his mind entirely on birds. Hunting raptors, particularly.

On his right shoulder, his greatcoat sported the most ridiculous epaulette she had ever seen: a large leather pad that flared well past the drop of his arm, giving his form an odd, asymmetrical cant that she could only see as hunchbacked. He was otherwise well-formed, but the strange dimensions of the coat he never seemed to remove marred his appeal irreparably.

The reason for the great leather epaulette wheeled above them as they rode, searching for prey. The hawk was a large example of its breed and, to Sonya's eye, in no way special save its unusual size. To hear the young Duke tell it, the bird was the most perfect expression of avian quality. It certainly ate and shat a lot.

Unlike most hunting birds she had seen, this bird never went hooded. Hand-reared from the egg, according to the Duke, it uncannily heeded his commands and seemed perfectly content to sit atop its leather perch on his shoulder rather than on the glove she had seen employed by other hawkers. The Duke never needed to deploy a lure to bring the bird winging back to him, simply clapping twice and giving a strange, trilling call that sat somewhere between a whistle and a scream to her ear. She could not imagine how the young Duke managed to create such a sound from a human mouth, but not only did he produce it with ease but it also never failed to recall the hawk to its perch on his shoulder.

Sonya preferred the times when the bird returned. When man and bird were in close proximity, they seemed to lose all connection to the world around them, communing with each other in coos and whistles and ignoring all around them. When the bird was off to hunt as it was now, the Duke hardly seemed able to contain his exuberance as he shared the his exhaustive knowledge on the subject of hunting birds. Whether his audience had any interest in his musings or not.

This expedition had been ill favoured from the outset and Sonya had only taken the commission after the Duke's family had doubled and then doubled again the already generous compensation offer. After a year spent defending a city she could hardly find on a map, Red Sonya of Rogatino had given in to her wanderlust and travelled west. Before long the need for coin had forced her to offer her skills once again in the service of those less inclined to wield weapons of their own. This most recent work had raised her hackles for more than one reason, but the promised coin had finally quieted her misgivings.

The Duke was betrothed to the daughter of a noble family that held grand holdings on the other side of the local mountain range. That range was home to any number of predators of the four- and two-legged-varieties. The mountain passes were also prone to rockfalls and the dangers of blizzard and flash flood, but none of that concerned Sonya overmuch. She had four stout swordsmen along and enough horseflesh to haul a tidy wagon that could shelter them all should the weather turn violent. The Duke rode in comfort within and each man rode a well-trained, surefooted warhorse bred for the mountains. The massive beasts were slow, but their presence was enough to give all but the largest of bandit bands pause.

Sonya's concerns were for what she had heard along her journey. The local lore was that a particular area of the pass they were meant to take held unnatural and unnamed dangers. The redhead feared no man, beast, or blade, but the terrors of the supernatural were another matter entirely. Her skill with blade and pistol was the match of any man alive, but ranging those skills against the undead was a challenge she did not relish.

For the moment, the horrors of lich and phantom were nowhere in sight as they gathered their little troupe, loaded supplies, and tacked the mounts. The young Lord, entirely oblivious to the labour expended about him, continued his unending lecture on the qualities and shortcomings of more birds of prey than Sonya had ever known to exist.

"In no way should you think I prefer the charms of the falcon, however. The gains of manoeuvrability and speed cannot be overstated, but no falcon ever took enough prey to feed the camp dinner!" laughed the Duke. That no one about him paid any attention or joined in his jocularity didn't seem to cause him any concern, and he launched into a new set of opinions with hardly a breath.

Sonya ignored the young dandy, flinging a water cask into the wagon with one hand as she kept a weather eye on the four young sides of beef she had commissioned for the journey. The two brothers, Lars and Sven were busy slinging saddles and fixing bridles. Neither spoke much of anything Sonya could decipher, but they each carried a flintlock rifle, a cutlass and a brace of pistols and looked as if they could use them well enough. Not quite twins, Lars seemed the older of the two blond, massive siblings, but they were easily confused for one another at a distance. They bickered and shoved one another as they worked, but work they did, and well enough that she left them to it.

She reserved her glares for the other two men. Older and lazier than the two young Swedes, Nikoli, a nine-fingered barrel of a man who had more food in his beard than in his pack and Yakhov whose teeth were as yellow as piss were older men and expert in the art of seeming to work while accomplishing little. Supplies moved but slowly under their care, and only

Sonya's relentless harangues and swats kept the two men from settling to rest completely. Somehow, eventually, they had everything loaded, the horses harnessed and the wagon rolling. To Sonya's great disgust, the sun was high overhead when they at last set out.

Sonya rode at the head of the little column, pointedly ignoring the eyes she felt tracking the roll of her hips in the saddle. Let them watch, so long as they kept their steel sharp and handy, it was a small price that she was willing to pay for their loyalty over the next few days. Should any think to shift from stares to caresses without her leave, Nikoli would not be the only man short of a digit.

Having consulted the Duke's best maps, copies of which were now rolled up in an oilcloth and tucked in a sealed tube that rode behind her saddle, she knew that they could make a decent campsite by just after nightfall. It would mean at least a short time travelling by torchlight, but thanks to their late start it was the best of their options. According to the chart, there was a small stream that ran cold but ice-free in all but the deepest depths of winter at a place where the path switched back sharply, some few hours up the trail. She urged her mount to greater speed without sparing a glance to see if the rest of the caravan kept pace. If her shrinking form wasn't enough incentive to spur their mounts, the dropping temperature and lengthening shadows should be. All of the men were experienced in travel in these parts and could read the signs as well as she.

Sonya had a small fire started in the clearing, her horse happily browsing on the scrub that grew around the stream. She had taken the time she had gained to take care of her bodily needs in private and now stood tapping an impatient foot as the rest of the column hove noisily into view. Between their torches and coarse laughter, every bandit in the hill country knew well that a fat prize had stumbled into their territory. She had hoped to get away with only forcing one man to each guard shift but that seemed a foolhardy risk now. She could fairly feel the hungry eyes watching from the heights.

"Get the horses untacked and build that fire higher, you dogs!" she shouted as the men dismounted. Set his nibs to a meal and then two of you to your bedrolls. Choose among yourselves who takes first and who takes last watch," she added.

"And the middle watch?" asked Nikoli, dragging his four fingered left hand through his knotted beard. The middle watch was the worst duty, requiring the splitting of sleep and leaving the watchers weary and bleary come morning.

"The midwatch is mine," she declared. The men looked at each other in astonishment. All had expected that one or more of them would be set to the duty. "I shall bed down by the carriage once I've supped. I sleep light and should I find any man dozing at his post we'll be traveling with extra mounts on the morrow," she warned. Without another word, she pulled dried meat and a loaf from her pack and set to. Washed down with clean mountain water, Sonya's meal was soon a memory, and she was asleep moments after folding herself to the ground and spinning a rough blanket around herself.

Sonya awoke before her watch and lay still in her bedroll, all her senses afire with warning. The wind shifted downslope, cold and metallic. An odd shushing murmur slid down the slope to her ears, nothing human in it. The horses stamped and blew. Sonya's eyes opened a sliver beneath her blanket. Something moved above, visible only when it blotted out stars as it passed, winged and silent.

She kicked her blanket aside and levered herself to a wary crouch. Her saber was within reach to her right but she pulled free one of her pistols and cocked the hammer before she reached down and slid the blade free. Light snoring came from within the carriage, and a more snorting, florid set of sounds came from the other side of the dying fire.

From where she crouched, she could see Lars, a pistol loose in one hand, sitting on a large boulder, his longsword resting across his knees. She could see he was not sleeping, his head cocked in an aspect that told her he, too, heard something nearby that had him wary and alert.

Assuming they were under hostile eyes, she deliberately made a show of rising and stretching theatrically. She strode slowly over to Lars and whispered his name. He nodded, casting his eyes up to alert her to what he heard. She nodded in return and then said loudly, unconcerned, "My watch, Lars. You and Sven..." At this she motioned by putting her hands to her head as a pillow to suggest that the two men should take their rest. Sven trotted up from the far side of the camp, his relaxed gait telling her that unlike Lars, he had not heard the strange noises.

Lars bent close and whispered to his countryman, then slapped the man soundly on the back and led him from the ring of light thrown by the dying campfire. Sonya heard the snorting, burbling sleep noises of Nikoli and Yakhov abruptly cut off, and a flurry of whispers came to Sonya's keen ears as the two Swedes hastily and quietly roused their comrades.

No sooner was her little band fully roused than the night erupted in fire and steel.

CHAPTER 04

In her time, Sonya had been the object of men's desires aplenty. She had been made gifts of flowers and sweets, fine silks and delicious perfumes in hopes of turning her head and opening her heart and her more intimate charms. In truth, no sweet fed her half so well as the ring of steel, no perfume fired her heart as the heady scent of powder smoke and primal fear. She trod a brace of delightful mountain flowers heedlessly underfoot as her saber turned a stroke intended to cleave her head from her shoulders. Red Sonya of Rogatino was more grateful for the tough leather corset she habitually wore over her rough-spun tunic than any fine silken gown. It turned a blade aimed at her kidneys by a man she hadn't sensed slithering up behind her. Her concentration had been entirely on the broken-toothed hill man with a notched sword and a dented buckler he used as a barge to push her back into the knife range of his fellow.

Finding herself suddenly with a foe before and behind, she chanced a shot with one of her precious pistols. In such a close and furious battle, she was unlikely to get the time to reload, so any shot taken must be worth the powder or the waste might prove fatal. She fired her left-hand pistol from the hip, blasting a ball into the gut of the reaver before her. He doubled over, and she hacked down hard on the back of his neck with her saber. She wrenched the blade from the man's spine, blood spraying and slopping in great fountains as she spun to the threat behind her. The little man who had stabbed at her kidneys backed furiously. Armed only with a small knife, he could be no match for this hellion and her two and a half feet of keen steel.

She could not let him escape to sheath his knife in another of her band.

Driving hard across the space between them, Sonya reached into the top of her boot with her offhand. One of her daggers crossed the space faster than her legs could carry her and buried itself in the little man's shoulder. She cursed her aim, never quite so sure with a thrown dagger from her left as she was throwing with her right. The slightly off-target throw was enough to bring the fellow up short as he clutched at the hilt of her blade with his other hand. The moment of distraction was enough.

She plucked her dagger from the corpse, wiping gore from the blade on the filthy rags that passed for the dead man's tunic. Across the clearing in the light of their little fire, she could see the shape of the battle. Something was very wrong.

Her men were handling the assault with relative ease, Lars chasing a man who carried a club that was little more than a stick with nails in it, splashing through the stream as the man fled. Sven was casting around for another opponent as his foe was down beneath the swing of his cutlass. Nikoli grappled with a man who apparently was trying to untether the horses where they had tied them for the night and Yakhov cradled his injured arm but no further assailants pressed that obvious advantage.

The carriage!

The whole damned attack was a feint. And like a raw recruit, she'd fallen for the ruse and let the pathetic little attack take her attention from the only thing of value they had with them.

The Duke's son.

The cry that came from the carriage froze her blood and brought the heads of every man in the clearing, mercenary or bandit, whipping round to the little wagon where it sat, tucked up against the rock face, its ornate decorations picked out by the light of the guttering campfire. The horses were picketed nearby and as a single entity they brayed and bucked, all trying to haul themselves free to flee. The cacophony only escalated as the eerie, unearthly cry sounded again, this time louder and longer. Inside the carriage another sound mingled with the strange, inhuman ululation. A very human scream.

Both noises suddenly and ominously were cut short. Sonya pounded furiously across the clearing, leaping gracefully over the fire and pitching headlong across the space between her and the ridiculous little carriage and its gaudy decoration.

She skidded to a halt as a massive, winged form emerged from the carriage, the solid shadow of it absorbing the firelight. A body tumbled lifelessly out of the little wagon ahead of the inhuman apparition, sprawling at Sonya's feet. She sucked in a grateful breath when she saw that the man on the ground was clothed in rags and dirt, his shaggy beard and balding pate obviously not the smooth cheek and coif of the young Lord Aldebrand.

The winged demon stood between Sonya and her charge and despite her terror of all things supernatural, Sonya raised her second pistol and took careful aim. What a lead ball might do to a thing not of the world of man she did not know. Effective weapon or no, Sonya would not leave the princeling to the hellish clutches of this winged devil. Not while there was yet a heart beating in her breast.

"Hold, Sonya," came the Lord's unnaturally calm voice from behind the spread wings of the phantom that menaced her. "This lady has saved my life this night," added the young man. His voice held surprising command, little like the babbling fool she had loaded into his carriage this very morning.

Reluctantly, she lowered her pistol. Not entirely, but enough that the weapon was not an immediate threat to the shadowed, avian form that stood atop the carriage, wings gently furling and unfurling as if to maintain its balance on a perch. Without warning, a smaller winged form erupted from behind the larger and Sonya almost reflexively put a ball into it. Some instinct stayed her hand and the Lord's massive hunting hawk flew like an arrow past her head so close she felt feathers brush her cheek. Next she knew, a scream rent the night behind her.

The hawk had driven a talon into the eye of a man who had escaped everyone's notice. He had crept up close enough that a short charge would have taken him into sword range of Sonya's unprotected back. The blade that clattered from his hand to strike sparks on the scree at the base of the rock wall made clear his intent.

Flapping and crying, the hawk tore at the man's face, one eye socket shockingly empty and spurting blood and fluid, his hands beating furiously at the air about his head but never managing to connect with the vicious, relentless feathered fury that tormented him.

By the time the Lord called his raptor to heel, the man lay moaning in the dirt, his hands clutched over his ruined face, his lifeblood seeping into the scrubby mountain grass that grew up in ragged tufts around the clearing. The stunning violence of the bird's attack had briefly taken everyone's attention from the strange figure atop the carriage.

When at last Sonya turned back to face the carriage, the strange winged apparition had vanished as if it had never been. All that told Sonya that she hadn't imagined the entire event was a faint shushing sound that came to her keen ears. The very sound that had awakened her just before the bandits' band hand launched its attack.

The hawk called out loudly and an inhuman but vaguely avian cry came to their ears from somewhere far, far above.

Sonya marched up to the carriage, and, grasping the Lord by the scruff of his lace and silken blouse, she heaved him bodily out of the carriage to sprawl gracelessly at her feet. His greatcoat tangled around his legs as he tried to salvage his dignity and leap to his feet, landing him in a heap on his bottom. Without waiting for his call, the hawk swooped down and settled contentedly on his shoulder, glaring at Sonya from its perch.

Sonya ignored the bird and fixed her glare on the young man still trying desperately to leap to his feet. She squatted before him and grabbed him by the lapels of his coat, tightening her grip until she had his full attention.

"Explain," she ordered with a growl and a violent shake.

CHAPTER 05

"An angel." Sonya's flat tone conveyed just how skeptical she was of this piece of intelligence.

"A woman with wings each wider than I am tall alit on the rail of my balcony on a moonless night. What was I to think?" asked Lord Aldebrand sheepishly. "That I kept my feet and my senses was almost as much as I could manage at the sight."

The men around her nodded sagely at this. Sonya was less impressed by the boy's explanation. "Nothing about that apparition spoke to me of Heavenly Hosts or a divine messenger. Just how much do you know of this 'angel'?"

"The Lady Raven is no angel, I've come to realize," he admitted. "Over the course of our acquaintance, I've realized that while her wings mark her as something beyond human, she is as much a part of our natural world as you or I."

"Does she bleed?" asked Sonya, cutting to the heart of the matter.

"I know not. I am certain that any who draw her blood, if it indeed flows as ours, would not live long to regret their action." He stroked his hawk's folded wing absently and then added, "Until meeting you, I had never met a woman so fearsome in aspect."

"Well and good," Sonya said, "but what is the creature after? Why track the caravan into the mountains?" She looked at the young Lord and asked with anger, "And why her interest in your Lordship to begin with?"

"Ah," began Aldebrand, "that is a sight more delicate than I care to share with...strangers."

Sonya looked around at her band of mercenaries and gave them a signal to leave her and the young Lord some privacy. She suspected she knew just what 'delicate' meant in this case and she felt for the shy lad. Deep in hostile country with only a handful of swords and a few horses, whatever menace this winged monstrosity posed outweighed her charge's modesty and she would have every scrap of information he knew before the sun rose.

"You will speak plainly of all you know of this 'Lady Raven,' my Lord," she said, her tone brooking no argument. "We are alone and but lightly armed in these mountains. If I am to keep you safe, I must know all there is of this before the morrow."

The young man sighed deeply and again reflexively stroked the flank of the bird that perched quietly on his shoulder. "The tale is passing strange and I fear I do not fathom much of what I have been told, but I will relate what the Lady Raven spake of her quest and my part in it."

Sonya simply nodded in encouragement. Around them, the men were saddling the horses and packing the camp, but this was of greater import than a quick start to the day. Her men knew their business and while they might not work as quickly without her supervision, the attack they had fended off would lend speed and vigour to their labours.

"The Lady Raven seeks some power that calls to her in her blood," Aldebrand began. "If I understand the tale, she came to our world from somewhere beyond our land, so far that she traveled in a great, powerful craft rather than by the power of her wings."

"A ship?" asked Sonya.

"Of a sort. I don't understand or quite believe, but this craft sailed the firmament, not the seas."

"It... flew?" Her question was both incredulous and fascinated. The idea was ridiculous. As ridiculous as a woman flying through the air on powerful wings each wider than she was tall.

"As I understand it," Aldebrand confirmed. "She pursued a rebel from the empire she served over distances I cannot credit. To hear the telling, she chased the villain from land to land for many years, never quite catching him up. Finally, she was able to get close enough to fire a broadside into his vessel but the same was true of him and both vessels were fatally wounded."

"And this happened nearby, in these mountains," she concluded.

"Actually, as I understand it, the battle happened so far up in the skies that the debris scattered across vast distances. The Lady Raven has retrieved pieces of her craft from locales not on any map in my father's study."

"And how is it that such a catastrophic battle could occur above our heads and this is the first I am hearing of such?"

"As I said, it is a tale that bids fair to strain all credulity. The Lady Raven claims that she and her quarry were marooned in our lands some tens of thousands of years ago."

Sonya gawped at him, not sure she had heard him correctly. "Tens of thousands of years?" she barked in disbelief.

"Aye," he answered with an earnest nod. "At first I could not credit it, but the Lady Raven is most convincing."

"And *old*, it would seem."

"To hear her tell it, those of her race are indeed long lived. Though not thousands of years long."

"Tens of thousands of years is longer than all of creation as I understand these things," grumbled Sonya. "So how is it this winged wench was loosing cannon-fire among the clouds before the Lord God made the world?"

"As I have explained, this tale stretches all that I know of reality, but were you to hear it from the lady's lips, you too would be convinced."

"And how do the lady's lips tell this tale of time beyond imagining?"

"The souls of her kind return to the world rather than ascending to the Lord's feet. Each time she and her foe die, they are born again to resume their endless war."

Sonya was dumbstruck. In her travels, she had met those who held beliefs that the faith of her own people would condemn as blasphemy. A lifetime of wandering, and encounters with creatures and forces beyond the ken of most had broadened her mind to allow that perhaps the world and the powers that controlled it were beyond even the teachings of the Bible. This lad spoke of something she had learned of in her wanderings among the dusky people of the Indus, well beyond the Arabias.

Reincarnation.

The idea had been fascinating and slightly terrifying to her at the time. An endless cycle of life, death, and rebirth that somehow locked two people into an eternal battle that could only lead to more of the same shook her to her core. That a soul might live eternally was foundational to her beliefs. That such a soul might be destined to an eternal struggle with an implacable foe struck her as more terrifying than any vision of hellfire and damnation she might conjure in her worst nightmares.

"By all the saints, your angel is eternally damned," she whispered, horrified.

"And well she knows it," he answered.

Shaking off the dread and spine-stiffening horror of the tale, Sonya brought her mind back to more immediate and present circumstances. "You say this Lady Raven seeks something she feels in her blood. Well and fair, but how do you figure into it? If some fragment of her ship lies in these mountains, why does she alight on your balcony rather than simply winging her way to the prize?" She suspected that she already knew the answer, but this labyrinth was as yet twisted beyond her ability to see her way clear. The details of the suspected dalliance might well cut the fog.

"Ah," Aldebrand stammered, colouring from his high collar to the base of his scalp. "That."

"That."

"These two winged beings have trodden the earth from time immemorial.

They live, they die, and they live again. But in between, sometimes they love." He cleared his throat and passed a hand absently over his hawk's flanks again. The gesture seemed to settle him. "As I understand it, Lady Raven can sense the lineage of her people in me, much the same as she senses the presence of some fragment of her craft in these mountains."

"The lineage of her kind. In you," Sonya said, thoughtfully. The young man's preoccupation with birds of prey and his uncommonly strong bond with his hunting hawk made a great deal more sense to her now.

Aldebrand caught the slightly salacious tone she injected into her comment and stammered his objection, "No, no. Nothing like that."

Sonya arched an amused eyebrow, saying nothing.

"My proximity was the merest coincidence. She was following tales of strange effects that linger where fragments of her vessel fell. As I understand it, the call of my blood to hers confuses her senses, making it difficult to follow that which calls to her from these mountains."

"I'm sure," Sonya smirked.

Aldebrand ignored the barb and continued, "That we travel in the direction of the power she seeks is also merest coincidence, but she came to me to warn me."

"Warn you," said Sonya flatly.

"There is danger ahead," he shrugged. "She was explaining it when the bandits attacked."

"And it was she, not you, who struck down the rogue in the carriage, yes?"

The boy didn't even have the sense to look sheepish as he nodded his confirmation.

"Danger ahead, bandits in the rocks, immortal women with wings," griped Sonya, ticking the items off on her fingers. She looked up at the young man, his attention already turning to his damnable bird. "The lout with the rusty sword might be roasting in hellfire, but he is laughing heartily while he burns."

“Beg pardon?” asked Aldebrand, catching only part of her complaint.

“Dawn breaks swiftly in the mountains. Be ready to ride when it does,” she said, hopping lightly to her feet and striding off to saddle her horse.

CHAPTER 06

The taller trees gave way to scrubby brush and a few tufts of the tough mountain grass as they climbed higher into the peaks. The higher they climbed, the colder it grew, as though the sun's strength thinned with the air." A sharp, bitter wind blew down from above, whipping Sonya's long red hair about her head like the leaping flame of a torch. She pulled a leather cord from the lacing of her tunic and tied her tresses into a thick tail that kept her vision clear. A few flakes of snow accompanied the bite of the gale, but the sky remained a bright, cloudless blue that hurt her eyes when she turned them up to it.

The young Lord Aldebrand had taken to riding one of their extra mounts this day and rode along beside her. His horsemanship was adequate she saw, but his main concern was for his hawk, not the beast beneath him. It wheeled above them even now, the mountains its natural hunting ground. Their journey would mean at least two more nights camping in the mountain passes and three days riding dusk to dawn besides. Her aching haunches envied the hawk's effortless gliding on the winds above.

The four men of her mercenary band rode in a loose box before and behind, the best she could manage with such small numbers of blades. Traveling alone, Sonya would have picked her way up a steeper path she had spied earlier, taking her out of the valley they now rode through. Even a few bandits might easily butcher them from above. The path she had seen was steep but manageable and the craggy cliffs could hide a dozen bowmen from sight as if they were made of smoke.

Her only advantage was speed and she pushed the little column as hard as she dared. After the night's events, even the lazier men goaded their mounts and took only the most urgent of rests to adjust tack or relieve their bladders. A mountain pass that had already proven to harbour hostile reavers was no place to linger.

"You fear ambush, Sonya?" asked Aldebrand quietly.

"Aye. As like as not, our dance partners were but a part of a larger band. If not in this vale by day, we will again be beset as we bed down tonight."

"We are in no danger, at least not at the moment," he said.

"Did your Lady Raven grant you the power to see the future?" she asked skeptically.

The young man looked up, shielding his eyes as he tracked the progress of his avian companion across the aching blue sky.

"Strelka knows," he said with a soft smile.

Sonya followed his gaze and squinted up at the circling raptor until it slipped out of view over one side of the peaks. She turned her gaze on the young Lord but said nothing.

Whether by chance or from some arcane communion with the hawk, Aldebrand's proclamation proved correct and they rode into the lengthening shadows without incident. Though they were not set upon, Sonya was not reassured.

As they stabbed deeper into the mountain range, the vegetation around them subtly changed. Not stunted as she expected of flora that clung to life high up in the peaks but twisted and somehow wrong in a feral, predatory way. The brush and scrub did not squat in fear of the wind but rather crouched, lying in wait for unwary prey.

A fox slunk through the shadows in her peripheral vision and flattened itself beneath the twisting limbs of a bush that had erupted in unappetizing black berries speckled a lurid red in irregular splotches. Sonya had the absurd urge to call a warning to the little creature, to warn it away from danger. As it disappeared beneath the shade of the brush, she half expected the gnarled branches to snap shut around the hapless creature. While the little dog-like animal emerged unscathed a moment later, Sonya could not shake the sense that it had only escaped doom by the barest of margins.

Even the usually oblivious Aldebrand noted the close, uncomfortable feeling that the more alert mercenaries and Sonya were experiencing. "The very rocks seem to watch our passing," he muttered, peering into the deepening shadows all around. Strelka, the great hunting hawk slammed down hard on the leather pad on his shoulder without warning. The men and even Sonya started at the shocking appearance of the bird, but Aldebrand did not so much as flinch at the mighty impact. He simply produced a gobbet of dried meat from a pocket and absently fed the creature.

It might have been a trick of the wind, but Sonya thought she heard the shushing sound of large, beating wings, though the only bird in sight sat placidly on Aldebrand's shoulder, its wings tucked neatly into their resting posture. She looked up but no motion broke the shifting light above her as the sun disappeared behind the crags.

"That clearing ahead," she ordered. "We make camp. This path is best not traversed by torchlight."

Once the camp was assembled and organized, a thin stew of dried meat and vegetables was ladled out to all, bread broken and passed around. Sonya set the same watches as the previous night and took herself to her rest. She lightly laid her thin blanket over her form, not rolling herself within as was her habit. There would be violence this night and she would not be tangled in a sheet when it struck.

Sleep took her swiftly and her dreams were of feathered phantoms, replete with bloody talons and hooked beaks.

Sonya awoke with a start, the sun warming her face. She had slept through her turn on watch. Worse, none of her men had roused her. She scrambled to her feet, her tousled scarlet mane flying about her like a blazing torch as she looked all about the clearing that had served as their campsite. Her senses refused to credit what she beheld.

Bodies. At least five men, though it was difficult to be sure as all had been rent apart like fowl at a feast table. Limbs were strewn about like windblown leaves, blood dripping from the stones and scree, thick with coagulation. Experience told her that these men had been dead for hours, yet she had heard nothing.

Impossible.

Across the clearing, the men of her band were rousing, equally staggered by the sight that greeted them with the dawn. All looked to her, but she had no answers. Two quick strides took her to the carriage. She feared what she might find within, but the young Lord was safely abed, snoring lightly.

Sensing Sonya looming above him, Aldebrand stirred and stretched as he rolled onto his back. The silken sheets, his tunic and his finely manicured hands were stained a deep, almost black shade of crimson. As he woke, he rubbed sleep from his eyes, leaving great round pits of red about his eyes.

The effect might have been comical if not for the dead men strewn about their campsite and the uncanny fact that all her swords and even she had slumbered while they died what could not have been quiet deaths.

The feel of the thickening blood on his hands and around his eyes made the young Lord blink. He gaped unbelieving at his hands, holding them away from himself as if wishing to throw them from him. His mouth opened and closed like a fish hauled from a stream, unable to form words in his shock.

Sonya's skin crawled as she realized that somehow, this popinjay had torn a handful of men limb from limb, apparently with his bare hands for she had not seen Aldebrand handle more than a spoon since they set out.

There was no earthly way one such as he might manage such a thing.

Magic.

A barely repressed shudder took her for a moment and all she could do was grip the sideboard of the carriage until she could wrestle the tremor to heel. Sonya might charge heedless into the teeth of a hundred swords or leap to the rolling deck of a ship crewed by a dozen pirates howling for her head and laugh with reckless joy at the danger, but magic was another matter. Though she had not seen the inside of a church in her adult life, she could still fear for her soul.

Lars slid up behind her, peeking into the carriage. His eyes grew saucer-wide when he spied Aldebrand's state. Crossing himself furiously, he shot off to his fellows, terror lending his limbs strength.

Damn.

"Are you wounded, my Lord?" she asked.

"Wounded?" stammered Aldebrand, not seeming to understand.

"The blood," she said, by way of explanation. "Is any of it your own?"

"My...blood...is...any...," and with a gulping sigh, the young Lord's eyes rolled back and he collapsed back into his bloodied linen.

Sonya gave a grunt and turned on a heel. She could hardly blame the boy for fainting. He had likely never seen a man bleed his lifeblood into the ground, let alone bathe himself to the elbows in it as he did. At least he would be no trouble for a while now.

Her men stood in a huddle, unconsciously finding the spot furthest from the remains of the men scattered around the clearing. Sonya kicked a hand from her path and nearly turned an ankle on an oozing pile that had been something foul before it was ripped from living flesh. Best to break camp and put this place behind them before Aldebrand awoke again. Once the morning sun got hold of all of this blood and effluvia, the stink would only get worse.

And where was his damned bird? Strelka was nowhere to be seen around the clearing nor in the skies above them. Though the hawk could hardly be responsible for the carnage all about her, Sonya could not help but imagine a connection between her strange avian dreams, the dismembered bandits and the missing raptor. Magic seeped from the very rocks all around them and it raised her hackles and made her teeth itch.

And what of this Lady Raven? Though not seen since that first shadowed glimpse on their first night in these craggy peaks, that winged apparition was at the heart of this debacle, Sonya was certain. It could be no coincidence that wings and talons had dominated her nightmare visions through a night of unnaturally deep slumber.

"Ho, dogs!" she called to her men. "Strike camp. I would be away from this foul place ere the sun climbs much higher. We drowsed long and ill this night. Let us make haste."

There was no argument and little discussion. Horses were tacked, bedrolls stowed and by unspoken agreement, they broke their fast on cold meat from their packs rather than heating a morning meal to be shared. She heard them talking quietly once they were moving up the trail and was disturbed to learn that visions of feathers, talons and bloodied beaks had visited all during their magically tainted sleep.

A few turns of the trail brought them into another switchback clearing where a stream had pooled into a cool mountain pond, stunted and gnarled brush hugging its banks. Sonya called a halt and gently roused young Aldebrand, leading him to the pond where he all but tore his bloodied blouse from his back. He scrubbed at his flesh long after the blood had washed away and Sonya and the men pretended not to notice his tears of horror.

Above them, the pumping, shushing of wings announced the return of Strelka. When Sonya turned to where her ears told her the bird had come to earth, she pulled up short. Not Strelka.

Lady Raven.

CHAPTER 07

"Something is amiss," said the winged woman without preamble as she plucked her helmet from her head.

Sonya watched as the massive wings that rose from Lady Raven's back folded neatly behind her. If she had not seen them retract, she might have assumed the woman wore some elaborate feathered cloak over her shoulders. The scale armour she sported was styled to resemble a cloak of feathers, jet black but shining with a metallic tint that tricked the eye into believing the scales flexed and rippled as true feathers.

Her helmet, now tucked casually under her arm, was exquisitely crafted to resemble a raven's head. The helm's individual quills were picked out in some of the most skilled metalwork Sonya had ever seen. The eyes were strangely covered by bright yellow glass, an affectation that seemed incredibly dangerous to Sonya's practiced eye. Glass lenses could easily be shattered and the shards could rip into the delicate flesh of an eye in an instant. The effect, however ill-advised, was startling. Until she removed the helm, Sonya had been convinced the woman had sported the head of a raven, the hooked bill hiding her full, sensual mouth from view.

"There is a gorge full of dismembered men an hour's ride down the mountain and some power beyond my ken stole my senses while it slaughtered them. My charge awoke awash in the blood of these men yet does not recall any part of the killing," said Sonya with heat. Punctuated by an eloquent gobbet of spit, she added, "Amiss."

"The leader, I take it," observed the Lady Raven with a surprised arch of her brow. "Rare to see a woman so elevated."

"Says the woman who flies like a bird," put in Nikoli from behind Sonya. Behind her back, she made a sign to warn him to stop his tongue, but she could not fault the wit of his observation.

"Fair point, warrior," conceded the winged woman with a chuckle. "The fact remains, something in these peaks has awakened and your cadre has not the knowledge or power to deal with it."

"Do you offer us your aid?" asked Sonya, working to keep the hope from her question. It was apparent that something with great power stalked the crags and she and her charges were little more than prey should it turn its attention to them. This woman, this angel or devil, might be a match for that power where Sonya and her fellows most certainly were not.

"To you?" asked the woman, her hauteur surging. "No." From the carriage, Aldebrand emerged, his hands and face scrubbed clean, a new blouse covering his chest. The haunted look had not been washed away as easily as the blood.

The Lady Raven lifted her mailed hand, the talon of her index finger pointing to the blinking noble as he awkwardly clambered from the decorated wagon. "I offer my aid to a fellow Tanaghaara. Only he is worthy of it." Sonya glared as the four mercenaries all choked back chortles with snorts and coughs. She could not disagree with the sentiment, but antagonizing the woman with the power of flight and fancy armour and weaponry seemed unwise.

"My Lady Raven," offered the young man with an unaccustomed bow, "these have saved my life but a night past, as you yourself did. I would consider it a kindness if you would enlighten us all. We travel as one and my heart tells me we might die as one among these peaks without your guidance."

Sonya glared back at her men, willing them to keep their peace. This creature, whatever her origin, was at the heart of the strange and horrible slaughter in their midst. Her power was obvious and if Aldebrand could convince her to wield it in their defence, Sonya would horsewhip any man who offered vexatious noises in disrespect.

"You truly are a son of Tanaghaara, though far removed in time and blood. Such loyalty does you honour, young Aldebrand," she said with admiration. "Very well, your company will have what aid I might offer. What you face in these haunted passes will face my steel as well."

"Steel did not rend those rogues to offal. They were torn apart, by forces I can scarcely imagine," said Sonya. The negotiation concluded, she would have answers if this creature had them to offer.

"In the distant past, this force was created by my people," explained the Lady Raven, "to serve us in battle."

"We are stalked by some phantom of your people? My understanding from Aldebrand," she threw a casual thumb over her shoulder to indicate the man still leaning against the carriage, his massive hawk perched lightly on his shoulder, "was that your craft and the energies it held were marooned here some thousands of years past. How might this 'force' menace us this day?"

"What is your name, firebrand?" asked the winged woman. "It has been many a lifetime since such heat and venom were cast directly into my teeth."

"Sonya of Rogatino," she answered, "and you have not explained how we are hunted by a power older than the mountains themselves."

"Your people still have not glimpsed the true scope of time. This power is old, older than most, but my people created these entities to use every means necessary to survive. Survive it has."

"And just what form does this power your people 'created' take?"

"It would have pulled life from what it could reach to sustain itself," explained the Lady. "See you? How the brush is stunted and twisted, the leaves speckled with corruption, the fruit bloated with cancerous lesions? A sure sign that what remains of the device lies close by."

"Device?" asked Sonya. "What you speak of is no trebuchet or cannon.

Your own words give it life and dank purpose."

"You would call it magic, Red Sonya of Rogatino," suggested the winged woman holding her eyes. "Whatever the name, thousands upon thousands of years, alone in these peaks, cut off from all contact and repair, have corrupted the intelligence that drives it. It no longer serves its intended function. What I can sense of it is disjoined, angered. And ravenous."

"Mad," observed Sonya. It was not a question.

"Aye, perhaps."

"A mad device of ravenous magic," called Yakov. Sonya glared at him afresh, but the man would have his say. "You drop from the sky to pronounce our deaths, Lady Raven."

"As a Valkyrie of Odin," intoned Sven, emboldened by his comrade's importune.

The winged woman smiled a grin that Sonya recognized, having seen its twin on her own mirrored features often enough. Battle flared hotly in her eyes as she answered, "And many a lifetime since I was so named, son of Ragnhar."

Sven and Lars both stiffened at her declaration and Sonya could see something like awe rise within the two Swedes.

"I carry weapons that may be effective against it," the Lady Raven said, "but they too are old beyond your measure. This thing was created to kill and it has had thousands of years to imagine its revenge for being abandoned."

"You would stand with us against it?" asked Aldebrand, striding unsteadily up beside Sonya. Strelka flapped her wings a bit to steady her perch as he moved. The winged woman gave an odd click and whistle and the great hawk launched itself from his shoulder to land upon her outstretched arm. Claws dug deep into the mail of her gauntlet but if the talons gave her pain, she showed no sign.

She stroked the bird's chest affectionately, nuzzling it to her chin and neck with more odd clicks and whistles. An unexpectedly girlish giggle squeezed from her lips as the hawk's lifting crest tickled her nose. She fixed Aldebrand with a look Sonya could not readily decipher and launched the bird back to him. "I will do what I can. I fear that what has been awakened might be beyond even my power to stop."

"Nothing in life is certain," said Sonya. "We have several hours of daylight ahead. Perhaps we can ride beyond the threat."

"You should try," answered the Lady Raven. Without another word, she unfurled her massive wings and launched herself into the air. Sonya felt an oddly hot gust on her upturned face as two powerful beats of those wings took the lady up and over the lowest peak and out of sight.

Looking up, Nikoli harrumphed loudly and grumbled, "Rude."

"Beautiful," suggested Lars with awe and not a little ardor.

"Terrifying," put in Yakhov as he goaded his mount to a walk.

"Impossible," added Sven, shaking his head as he threw a leg over his saddle.

Gently escorting Aldebrand back to his carriage before mounting her own steed, Sonya could not disagree with any of them.

CHAPTER 08

The sun passed overhead and Sonya noticed that sometime shortly before it set their progress shifted to a subtle downward track. It might be a trick of the mountain's geography, but a glance at the map she kept rolled in the tube behind her saddle told her that in all likelihood they were on the downslope of the pass. The climb was over, and only a day's travel would take them clear of the peaks.

Before then, they must either camp another night among the haunted heights or risk travel by torchlight over unfamiliar and fractured ground. Alone and unhindered, Sonya would have pushed on but with four weary companions and an awkward carriage hauled by two high strung stallions the path was simply too dangerous to risk with only torches to light the way.

Sonya did not rebuke her men for building the camp's fire far larger and brighter than was wise in a territory marbled with bandits and cutthroat mountain men. The true danger to them would not come from swords or musket fire. The blaze might not keep the monstrous power at bay, but it did offer comfort while they waited. There would be no watch tonight, for none but Aldebrand had the least interest in retiring to the bedroll.

From his pack, Sven produced an instrument, something between a lute and a poet's harp and strummed it absently. Lars began to sing in a language Sonya had only a few words of. Sven quietly translated his song in a rhythm the two had obvious practice at. Lars would sing his haunting lyric, and then Sven would repeat it while strumming the same pattern on his odd instrument.

Let sword-bearers listen, while I recount feats of
weapon-points concerning Haraldr the exceedingly wealthy.
I shall recount the words that I heard a white,
bright-haired girl speak when she spoke with a raven.

The valkyrie thought herself wise;
men were not pleasing to the aggressive maid,
who understood the voice of the bird.
The white-throated and the bright-eyelashed one
greeted the skull-picker of Hymir the Raven
which sat on the edge of a cliff.

What is the matter with you, ravens?
From where have you come
with gory beaks at break of day?

Flesh hangs from your claws;
the stench of carrion comes from your mouths;
I think you lodged last night
near where you knew corpses were lying.

The grey-feathered sworn-brother of the eagle,
Lady Raven gloated and wiped its bill,
and gave thought to an answer:

We have followed Haraldr son of Hálfdan,
the young king, since we emerged from the egg... *

The effect was hypnotic and Sonya was grateful for the distraction. The song might bode ill, but the music and the comfort of it were welcome. As the stanza trailed off, a scream rent the night from somewhere near the carriage. It reminded Sonya of the strange, ululating cry that Aldebrand used to summon Strelka, but the flavour of it was pain and terror.

All turned as one to the carriage, expecting the young noble to toss himself out in fear at the sound, but what emerged was neither fully Aldebrand nor in any way fearful. In the wavering torchlight, Sonya saw the apparition raise a hand to them, a loaded flintlock held steadily at her chest. The hand was attached to no arm at all, simply floating in midair. The stump of his arm showed flesh and bone to her astonished eyes in the flickering light of the bonfire. Part of his face was missing, the upper jaw and one cheek absent, his tongue and lower teeth exposed in the unhinged jaw that hung below his nose.

He moved with certainty and purpose she had not seen in his gait previously, dropping lightly from the carriage to balance on the balls of his feet. One leg also had vanished, though the foot below it trod the earth as sure as ever. Sonya blinked furiously, fearing that what she was seeing was some trick of the light and fire, not the magic she feared.

Stunned by the terrifying sight of half a man bearing down on her, Sonya hesitated a hair's breadth too long and the young noble squeezed the trigger of his flintlock. If not for the shocking impact of a winged apparition dropping thunderously onto his back in that instant, she would have folded around the ball in her death spasm. As it was, the lead sphere punched through her scarlet mane, ripping loose a lock of hair as it passed.

The crack of the powder and the heat of the close miss shook Sonya from her reverie and she leapt to follow up on the lady's strike. Aldebrand had discarded the spent pistol and came at her with clawed hands upturned, what remained of his face a snarling rictus of rage. As she closed, she slapped a hand hard onto where his wrist ought to have been out of instinct and was surprised to meet exactly the flesh and cloth she expected. To her eyes, her hand grasped nothing whatever, but she could feel the sinew and bone in her grip.

She attempted to twist him over a hip to take him from his feet, but using unaccountable strength, he reversed her grip and effortlessly tossed her across the clearing to slam against the carriage. She knew nothing else until her eyes fluttered open in weak morning light, the Lady Raven silhouetted above her.

With difficulty, she propped herself up on her elbows, wincing at the light as it awoke a pounding hammerstrike rhythm in her temples. She reached a hand up and gingerly prodded at the back of her head through the mass of tangled hair. The hand came away bloody, but there didn't seem to be more than a small cut in her scalp above an apple-sized lump of tender flesh. She would live.

More's the pity, she thought as the hammer blows redoubled as she sat upright. "What in the nine hells?" she demanded. The Lady Raven rested a hand on her shoulder and gave her a squeeze that Sonya thought might be in comaraderie or reassurance. She took nothing from the gesture.

"You survived the night, Red Sonya of Rogatino," said the winged woman flatly. "Your men fared less well."

"My men..." Sonya asked weakly, fearing the answer.

"Not all of us are dead," chimed in a surprisingly cheerful voice. "Lars, Sven and I live," said Nikoli. "We buried poor Yakhov, best we could." He gestured at a man sized cairn that hunched unnaturally at the bottom of a sheer cliff, stones piled upon lonely ground to mark the end of the man.

"Though I suspect Lars might wish it otherwise," added the Lady Raven. Sonya followed her nod to see Sven tending to the other Swede as he lay near the remains of their campfire. She could see that Sven's arm was bound up and slung and his stiff, pained movements told her that he had not escaped the night's battle unscathed. Lars did not seem to respond to his war brother's attention at all.

Seeing what she saw, Nikoli said, "He lives. Not a life any would choose, but he lives."

Sonya did not ask for an explanation but pushed her unwilling body from the ground and crossed the distance to the two Swedes. The form lying prone at Sven's feet was Lars in name only. His flesh had somehow been pulled taught to his bones, the once muscular chest and handsome features now a flesh-bearing skeleton and little more. His eyes lolled in his head and tiny, pitiful moans escaped his gasping mouth. Sven looked up into Sonya's eyes, tears welling in his.

"That...thing. It latched onto him and even as I tried to reach them, it pulled his life from him." The hulking Swede sniffed back a sob and swiped his uninjured hand across his overflowing eyes. "Before I could strike, Lars was as you see him."

Nikoli slid up behind Sonya and peered down at the near lifeless man on the ground. "Sven here lopped off the bastard's hand halfway to the elbow, but he hardly broke stride. Just snatched up the severed hand, bounded over the rocks, grabbed poor Yakhov as he was reloading and did the same to him."

"Your man here," added the Lady Raven as she joined the little group at their dying fire, "put a ball into him from but a few yards away. It slowed him not at all."

"Yakhov was dead before I could get within a sword stroke of the fiend," said Nikoli. "Tore off into the night like his arse was alight. We could not rouse you, but you didn't seem killed, so we tended you as best we could, bound up this Swede and hoped the devil would not return."

"So far, we have seen nothing of young Aldebrand since," said Sven. "Though 'tis a certainty he lies close."

"A certainty?" asked Sonya.

Nikoli pointed up and Sonya saw that above them, Strelka was gliding in a long, lazy circle. "She hasn't roosted since the sun climbed above the peaks, nor has she moved on."

"Strelka watches over him," said the Lady Raven. "Hawks can be fiercely protective."

From the ground, a choking gurgle arose weakly and Lars sputtered his last. Sven gently closed his staring eyes, muttering a blessing or prayer Sonya chose not to hear. There would be time for grief if what remained of her band managed to escape the mountains before whatever had possessed Aldebrand took their lives the same way. With a nod and a point, she detailed Sven and Nikoli to erect a second cairn for the man. While they worked, she ushered the Lady Raven out of earshot.

"How do we fight this?" she asked, bluntly. "And can we free Aldebrand from its clutches or must he die to end this?"

From across the clearing, Sven's strong tenor sang out, accompanied by the plucks and strums of his odd little harp. He sang in Sonya's tongue, the song for the living, not the dead.

The slain lay there on the sand,
dedicated to the one-eyed embrace-occupier of Frigg;
We welcomed such doings. *

The last strains of his lament echoed across the peaks, and Sonya hoped they reached the ears of the All-Father the two men revered. Though she did not share their strange faith, the warrior in her understood it, perhaps better than her own. The gentleness of the faith she had been raised in had always warred with her nature. The warrior gods of the north and the songs of their deeds stirred her as none of the tales of her childhood ever had.

Her head cocked in a decidedly bird-like gesture, Lady Raven listened to the song and said, "These men could be of Tanaghaara. Warriors and poets."

"And Aldebrand?" asked Sonya.

"He bears the blood of my people, perhaps even my own. That is why the spirit has taken him. It senses that blood and can connect to it."

"Does ought of the boy remain within or is he merely a vessel?"

"You see the heart of the problem, though the science of it can only be beyond you," observed the Lady Raven, her wings rustling as she stood watching the two mercenaries pile rocks upon their comrade's lifeless form.

"Magic is the heart of the problem, whatever name you place upon it," said the redhead, unable to keep the heat from her voice. "And you have not said if we might yet save young Aldebrand or if we must name him among the dead in the accounting of all this."

The feather motif armour rippled and flexed like no metal Sonya had ever seen as the woman twisted around and pulled a slender dagger from a sheath strapped to her thigh. Flipping it to offer the hilt to Sonya, she said, "If the boy can be saved, it will mean cutting his connection to the spirit that has usurped his will. This blade was forged in the fires of my homeworld, of metal not found in this realm. It will serve where your weapons will not."

Taking the hilt, Sonya noted an odd warmth that seemed to emanate from the metal of the blade. The blade shimmered oddly, as if the colour could not settle on a single aspect. Looking at it too long was strangely disconcerting. She raised her eyes in a question to the winged woman. "To free Aldebrand or to kill him?"

"In his place, would you wish to live if you could not be freed of the spirit's influence?" asked the Lady Raven, her gaze leaving no question in Sonya's mind of which fate the winged woman would choose.

Sonya tucked the oddly warm dagger behind her belt in the small of her back. It wasn't much of a weapon, but if it could affect the entity when pistol balls couldn't, it was worth keeping close to hand. That and the knowledge that Sven's blade had still hacked through Aldebrand's wrist gave her hope that they might yet rescue what remained of the young noble.

"The boy is still close," said Sonya, gesturing to the circling hawk above them. "If the spirit that animates him drains the living for its sustenance, it isn't likely to let three more meals escape without a fight."

"You would bait the snare yourself?" asked the Lady Raven, eyeing the circling raptor thoughtfully.

"My charge was to see Lord Aldebrand over the mountains. The Duke will have sent a bird to his cousin. Should I arrive without the young Lord in hand, my life will not be worth the price of one of his shiny buttons." With a sigh, she added "And for all his foppishness, the boy does not deserve the fate he has been dealt. I would free him if the chance remains."

"Another warrior cut from Tanaghaara cloth, Red Sonya of Rogatino," chuckled the Lady. When Sonya shot her a glare, she waved her hands and added, "No, I do not sense that you are of the blood as Aldebrand. I only commend your honour and spirit, not your lineage."

Striding up to the two women in time to hear the last few moments of their exchange, Nikoli looked both women up and down before adding, "Do not judge with such haste, fair Sonya. I think the wings might suit you."

CHAPTER 09

Every eye watched the heights. Every nerve taut, expecting an attack at any moment, the journey taxed them in a few hours far more than all the previous leagues had. The three of them were nearly spent when the rocky terrain and stunted vegetation began to open out into green and rolling hills below them.

From above, the haunting, ululating cry sounded again and Nikoli was suddenly slammed to the ground, bones of wrist and ankle snapping violently with the impact. Sonya instinctively whipped one of her pistols up and fired into the attacker's center but whatever magic protected it shrugged off the impact as if she had thrown naught but a piece of rotten fruit.

Sonya and Sven leapt from their mounts, both hitting the flailing, struggling mass that rolled across the trail. Nikoli's screams of rage and terror had grown weaker even within the moments between Sonya's first volley and her leap. Through the missing pieces of Aldebrand's body, she caught a glimpse of the mercenary's face, the flesh shriveling to a rictus of horror even in the instant her flying form slammed into the two of them. Sven landed atop her a moment later and there was a chaotic struggle as the tangle of limbs wrenched and flailed.

With a violent kick, Sonya booted Aldebrand off the still body of Nikoli. His staring eyes and shriveled flesh revolted her but she ignored them and focused on her opponent. Sven rolled on the ground, possibly injured and too far from her to be of immediate assistance. For the first time, she got a good look at Aldebrand in the fading light of day.

Sven claimed to have lopped off one of the boy's hands, but whatever evil had possessed him had either reattached or regrown the hand. She could see that his limbs were not disconnected as they had appeared to her in the first attack. The guttering light of their fire and the strange magic that was affecting the young noble had tricked her senses and she could see now that the magic somehow turned random segments of his form clearer than any glass. Sonya did not have the words to describe the effect but at least her brain was able to understand it as some kind of illusion, not some magic that animated disconnected flesh.

Illusions could not harm her.

Still, the horror of watching this young man possessed hit like a physical blow. The power that had taken him was like nothing she had seen, though many strange and fantastic things had befallen her in her travels. This was evil on a level that she had not known possible, the taking of not just the body from the boy but his whole self, his very soul. She was repulsed by what it could mean that such a usurpation was possible. The Lady Raven had been correct. Though it might mean her life, she could not leave Aldebrand to such a fate.

Another strange cry came to her ears and the hurtling form of Strelka slammed down onto Aldebrand from above. Sonya could not credit the hawk attacking the young man, unless it somehow sensed the evil that overtook him and was in its way trying to defend him from it. Wings and talons beat about his head, distracting him long enough for her to reach Sven's side and lift the mercenary unsteadily to his feet.

"We have to get him back into the rocks. Box him in."

Sven looked at her in horror, "You want to go back into the pass? We can fight him on open ground!"

"He is too strong! Whatever evil attacks his soul has leant power to his limbs. You felt it when he shrugged us off like gnats."

"And you want to put his back to a wall? You are mad, woman!" As he ran for his mount, he called back, "I have always fancied the mad ones!"

"Shut up and *ride*!"

Still ineffectually beating at the clawing, rending talons, wings and beak of the hawk, Aldebrand could not stop either of them as they mounted and galloped back into the craggy rocks that defined the opening of the pass on this side. Though she could see through parts of him, where it didn't hold close to his body, the oversized greatcoat swirled and flapped around him like an animate shroud.

Over her shoulder, she saw the hawk finally give up its assault and launch itself back into the air. The form of Aldebrand swiped blood from its face and pounded after them. She urged her mount to greater speed, hoping there was time to reach the killing ground she and Lady Raven had scouted earlier that day.

"Follow, young Lord. I would see you find your marriage bed," she said to herself as she leaned over the horse's neck and urged it onward.

Another look told her that incredibly, the man was keeping pace with the riders, though he had only the power of two legs to propel him. Even as she watched, the distance between them narrowed slightly, his arms and legs pumping relentlessly. The cliffs grew higher as they pounded back the way they had come, driving deeper into the pass. The ambush point was just ahead. They could make it.

Should they survive this desperate gambit, she could apologize to Sven then. There had been no time to give him the shape of their plan. She simply had to hope that he was the professional swordsman she believed him to be. One or the other of them would be the entity's target when they split up and if the thing chose her to pursue, she needed Sven to do his part without instruction.

Foam flew from her mount's lips and its metal shod hooves raised sparks when they struck stones on the trail. The beast's heaving breath and pounding hooves raised an almighty clatter as they drove into the pass. Sonya's hair flew behind her like a trailing blaze, lacking only smoke. The scabbard of her sword slapped her thigh in time to the rise and fall of the horse's withers and she mercilessly snapped the reins to urge the beast on. The light was failing and she needed to see the damned thing coming if they had any hope at all.

Until she had met the Lady Raven, a full gallop such as this had seemed to Sonya the pinnacle of speed, bordering on flight itself. Now she found herself wondering what the winged woman must experience as she carved the sky. A shame there wasn't a way to don such a pair of wings of her own.

A wave and a point instructed Sven to peel off. The trail widened out here and then closed back in up ahead. She planned to box the creature in where the trail narrowed and if Lady Raven did her part, they might be able to overpower the monster and bring it to the ground. If they could do so without seriously harming Aldebrand, all the better. She doubted they could manage it without harm to themselves.

Behind her, Aldebrand was closing the distance. No man could outrun even a slow horse, but the magic that possessed the boy lent his limbs impossible power and speed. He did not even appear to be breathing heavily.

Her mount sensed the danger closing in on its haunches and found a deep reserve of speed of its own. Though death beat a rhythm behind them, the wind in her face brought a grin to Sonya's lips. The thing had chosen her for its prey and ignored Sven and his fleeing mount.

Good.

The agreed upon place was just ahead. Sonya vaulted from her mount, rolling gracefully to absorb her momentum. She landed on her feet and pivoted with the last motion of her roll to face the enemy. Her steel leapt into her right hand, a loaded pistol into her left as she dropped to a pantherish crouch. Aldebrand pounded across the shrinking distance, most of him visible, but parts of his face, his torso and his arms and legs apparently lost to the magic that enveloped him. The effect distorted her aim.

The ball impacted him on his shoulder rather than his chest, but whatever sorcery mazed the sight of him also protected him. He shrugged off the impact without slowing. He held no weapon, but she had seen the effects of his magically augmented strength in the strewn-about remains of the bandits slain by his hands the night before. She could not afford to underestimate him, armed or not.

Another shot rang out behind the onrushing apparition. Sven's pistol. His aim was truer than Sonya's had been, but the effect was no greater. The ball slammed into Aldebrand's back, the flattened ball tinkling musically to the stones as its energy was somehow absorbed by the power of the magic enveloping him. With only her sword between her and the avalanche of power bearing down on her, Sonya could not help but wonder if even a cannon would be enough to stop the evil she faced.

An inhuman cry sounded and reverberated off the low cliffs, presaging the driving, punishing strike of Lady Raven from the heights. She slammed bodily into Aldebrand's running form, forcing him from his feet into an awkward, flapping roll, his greatcoat whipping around him, bringing him into full focus for the first time since the battle had begun. The effect was short-lived and when he found his feet parts of him once again began to disappear from view at random. Now that she was close, Sonya could see that some sort of material had enveloped him beneath his greatcoat, clinging to him like wet linen. There was even a film over his face, distorting what she could see of it when it was visible.

"The knife, Sonya!" called the Lady Raven as she wheeled in a tight roll above the trail. The canyon was narrow, forcing her to make hard, flapping turns. Sonya saw her tuck her wings and drop as she came too close to the cliff face. She recovered but could not turn quickly enough for another strike. "On his arm! There's a kill switch!"

"A what?" Sonya called, dancing back as Aldebrand reached for her.

"I recognize the suit now! On the left arm there's a panel. It will have a cover."

"His arm? Are you mad woman?" called Sven, galloping his horse into the tight confines of the trail. He held his other pistol before him and when he was only a few body lengths from Aldebrand, he fired. At the closer range, the impact had a greater effect. The ball again flattened and clinked to the stones, but the shot staggered the boy, raising a cry of pain from him as he lurched forward to catch his balance.

Sven swiped a wild backhand as he thundered past, but Aldebrand's reeling form evaded it. He lashed out at the passing mercenary in return, catching the horse on its rump with a strike that spun the animal off its hooves, throwing Sven bodily into the nearest cliff face. The impact made a sickening, soft crunching sound and Sonya couldn't be certain if the swordsman yet lived, so violent was the collision. At the least, he would be of no further aid in this battle.

His horse rolled, snorting and protesting to its feet. Riderless, instinct and fear drove it deeper into the pass, away from the creature who had caused it pain. Sonya could not fault the impulse.

Spying that the wheeling, swooping form of the Lady Raven was lining up for a new attack, Sonya changed her own tactics. She had to now be giving ground, letting Aldebrand push her back into the tighter part of the pass, where the cliffs were almost close enough together that a large man might touch both at once, just by reaching out his arms to either side. Now she wove a web of steel, slicing at the boy's arms and hands as he tried to grapple with her. Though the strange fabric that swathed him seemed to protect him from the power of a pistol ball, she was able to slice through it and draw blood with her blade.

It was difficult to tell, but it appeared that the fabric, once rent would inexplicably heal itself and Aldebrand almost instantly, for there was little blood after the initial release. Still, her steel was enough to hold the creature at bay, if only barely. Over its shoulder, she spied the plummeting form of Lady Raven, a studded club that somehow carried a glow about it in her mailed fist. She struck the boy soundly on the temple as she speared past him, the gust of wind from her wings buffeting Sonya from her feet.

Again staggered, Aldebrand reeled, clutching his head. An instant later, Sonya watched him shrug his massive greatcoat from his shoulders. A pair of wings, perhaps half the size of Lady Raven's own, unfolded from his shoulders. She could see the pain on his face as they ripped free of the clinging fabric and he flexed them experimentally. A mighty leap took him aloft and a mad, frantic flapping gained him altitude until he was atop the cliff.

The Lady Raven slammed to the ground beside the sprawling form of Sonya. She scrambled to her feet, swiping her sword from the ground as she rose. "He has wings?" she cried, incredulous.

"It would seem he does," answered the winged warrior, straightening her raven helm and rolling her shoulders as her wings settled into what Sonya recognized as a ready, but resting posture.

"And how in the nine hells do we fight a man with wings?" she demanded of her uncertain ally.

The Lady Raven's wings snapped open and she reached out to enfold Sonya in an embrace. "Fire with fire, Red Sonya of Rogatino."

CHAPTER 10

Sonya had once been charged to rescue the daughter of a merchant from slavers. The girl was nubile and comely but not easily pliable. To keep her cooperative and thus profitable, they had plied her with drink and the smoke of hashish. When Sonya had found her in the tent they had kept her in, the air was thick with the spicy, pungent vapour. Sonya had inhaled much of it in the effort to rescue the girl and slay her captors, leaving her with both a foggy consciousness and an odd fluttering lightness in her belly that took hours to pass.

The same strange giddiness filled her now, though this was of greater intensity by any measure she could name. A raw sound tore from her throat unbidden, something between a yell of fury and a whoop of joy. Looking down, she knew she ought to fear the fall, but the thrill of impossibly falling upwards only brought a feral grin to her features.

The Lady Raven held her firmly, meeting her eyes as they drove up to the heights. "You may have some blood of Tanaghaara in you, Red Sonya of Rogatino. I have taken a handful of humans aloft in my time, but none before you enjoyed the experience."

"In my life I have stood on the prow of the fleetest ship as it was driven before a gale, leapt from the saddle to meet the enemy and even been thrown from the parapets of a besieged city. This?" Sonya shouted to make herself heard over the rush of the wind in their faces. She met the lady's eyes through the strange yellow lenses of her helmet and yelled, "This above all!"

Sonya thrust her hands above her, embracing the sky as they rose. "If I die this day, you have given me a gift I can never repay!" she finished, adding another wordless whoop in punctuation.

With a laugh, the Lady Raven snapped her wings and added a burst of speed, aiming for a landing atop the cliff but beyond Aldebrand's immediate reach. He had crumpled to a heap as he reached the summit, his vestigial wings driven past their limit, apparently.

"He probably won't be able to fly again. The armour augmented his wings to let him escape, but he is no full-blooded Tanaghaara. It will have cost him," the winged warrior shouted as they made their landing.

Sonya reluctantly stepped from the woman's embrace and turned to their foe. She drew the strange dagger from behind her belt and held it to the last of the day's light, watching the metal glint and waver unnaturally. "And we need to use this 'kill switch' you spoke of," she said, half a question.

"Aye. On the left arm there is a panel. Beneath the cover there is a set of controls. One of them should..." She grasped for the words to fit the concept to Sonya's experience. "One of them will drain the magic from the entity."

"One of them?" Sonya asked, concerned. "There is more than one of these...controls? How can we know which to use?"

"I fear I cannot say which. It has been a hundred lifetimes since I trained in this art."

"Wonderful," murmured Sonya, shifting the dagger to her left hand. She rolled her shoulders and swung her sword in an angry arc to loosen her wrist. The blade might not be enough to stop Aldebrand, but it was her only true weapon. The dagger would only come into play if she was close enough for him to grapple with her and the cyclopean strength the magic lent his limbs made the prospect one she wished to avoid.

"The blade may be small," said the Lady Raven falling into step beside her, "but it is a mono-molecular edge..." When she saw the questioning look in Sonya's eyes she added, "and it carries powerful magic of its own. It may be the only instrument capable of opening the panel on his arm. Keep it close."

Sonya nodded her understanding.

"You just keep hitting him with your magic mace. I will try to get in close and use this," she waggled the dagger, "unless he rips my arms off first."

"Best to avoid that," said the winged lady as they clambered over the uneven ground of the clifftop.

At that, they were atop Aldebrand. He crouched in waiting, an animal at bay. The young noble fop she had escorted from his father's house was little in evidence. The stubby wings were folded against his back. The mottled, visible, and transparent aspect of his face and limbs shifted and flowed like oil on the surface of a still pond. His face, distorted by the clinging film of the magic that enveloped him, stared back blankly, the lack of emotion more terrifying than any howling rage Sonya had ever faced.

"Aldebrand," she said quietly, approaching him cautiously. "Let me help you."

The young Lord stared back without reaction. She could see no recognition in his eyes, no trace of the lively fop who had regaled her with endless useless facts about his beloved birds of prey.

Without a word, he launched himself at them. Lady Raven stepped before Sonya, snapping her wings open protectively. Sonya did not see the swing but clearly heard the impact of the winged woman's glowing mace on flesh and bone. A muffled grunt and the sound of a body hitting the ground swiftly followed the blow.

When the wings blocking her view furled back over the woman, Sonya saw that Aldebrand was already recovering from the strike. Sonya leapt and closed the distance, placing the tip of her sword at the base of the boy's throat before he could rise. "Stay down, pup," she ordered.

Viper quick, his hand shot up and grasped her blade at the midpoint. A wrench and a snap followed in lightning succession, his hand coming away bloody but holding an arm's length of steel. Sonya looked at the hilt of her fine steel cutlass and the handspan of blade that remained. A ringing clatter announced that he had tossed the rest of her weapon aside.

"Damn," she growled.

She aimed a blow at his head with the dagger in her offhand and was shocked when a swath of the clinging fabric fluttered away, revealing the bloody face of the young man beneath. The weapon might have magic at that, she thought.

"Help me, Sonya..." came a weak plea, the first indication she had that the boy yet lived within the enveloping, cloying magic.

The Lady Raven swung her glowing mace and connected solidly with the boy's shoulder from behind. The blow took some of the vigour from the boy and Sonya was able to grasp his wrist. The winged woman closed and took hold of his right arm with both of her hands, letting the mace fall from her grasp to dangle from her wrist by a metallic cord.

As she tried to lever the dagger point against his weakly struggling arm, she saw a raised oval on the fabric that looked harder and more metallic than the rest of the film that clung to him. She aimed the point at it, unsure how it might open. The blade slid smoothly into the harder material and the entire oval cover snicked off and bounced away into the darkness. Beneath the covered section, a constellation of lights blinked in a myriad of colours. Sonya blinked, unsure of what she was seeing. To her it looked like the lights she saw behind her eyelids after a severe blow to the head and it made as much sense.

"What do I do?" she shouted, ashamed of the panic she could hear in her own voice.

"There's a button, something raised on the panel! Blue, I think..." As the Lady Raven was about to explain further, the entity found a reserve of energy and with a heave, tossed the winged woman bodily up and away from it. Sonya heard bones snap as the woman rolled off the edge of the cliff. That she did not immediately swoop back up onto the peak told Sonya that the bones that had loudly cracked might have been in the lady's wings.

The arm Sonya held flexed beneath her hands and she braced herself for a similar attack. In desperation, she slammed her hand against the lights that rippled and roiled on the fabric. She felt a *something* raised beneath her fingers, and without knowing if it was the right thing to do, she stabbed it, hard.

For a moment, nothing at all happened. Then Aldebrand screamed, but it was not his voice that erupted from his throat. A burbling, tearing sound, it reminded Sonya of nothing so much as the rending of metal. Metal that could feel pain.

The clinging fabric fell away from the young Lord in sheaves, like the petals of a dying rose. After a few moments, all that remained of the mystical garment lay lifeless beneath the unconscious Aldebrand. It appeared as nothing more than a shredded linen garment. She crumpled a bit of it in her hand and could feel nothing but simple fabric.

The young Lord Aldebrand's eyes fluttered open and he looked up at the stars, breathing slowly. He levered himself to his elbows and faced her. "Sonya?" he asked, puzzled. "Where am I?"

Strelka swooped down and landed in her customary place on his shoulder. Without the thick leather pad, her talons dug into his flesh, blood welling instantly around the sharp points of her claws. Sonya winced for him but he seemed not to even notice, reaching up and absently running a knuckle from her throat to her belly affectionately.

"What do you remember?" asked Sonya, genuinely curious.

"We made camp and once we had supped, I turned in. It was a hard ride yesterday, trying to put distance between our first camp and tonight's.

"That was yesterday. You don't recall the events of that night and the next day?"

"Nay. I only recall thinking how glad I was that we had only this morning's ride before we cleared the pass," he explained. He looked down at his state of dress, his shredded clothing and the welts on his arms and hands. He held his hand up before him, turning it about as if seeing it for the first time. "What has happened?"

"What..." Sonya began. From below, a clamor arose, interrupting her thoughts. A glow of torches weakly reached out of the canyon and from the raised voices, Sonya realized that a band of mountain bandits had come upon their discarded mounts. She heard Sven's unmistakable Swedish cursing and a cry that could only have come from the lips of the Lady Raven.

And all she had to work with was a dagger and a broken sword.

CHAPTER 11

Aldebrand pushed his head over the side of the sheer cliff, joining her as she assessed the assailants below. The Lady Raven had indeed broken a wing and sat with her back against the far wall of the gorge, the wing at a sickening angle. She was in no shape to fight and Sven had already been bound hand and foot. Four of the five men she could see were enjoying the sport of kicking and shoving their captive. The fifth was busy rifling through the meager belongings they had carried in their saddlebags.

From her elevated vantage, she could easily have put a musket ball in each of them, but her pistols had been spent during the fight, and her powder and shot were all stowed in her packs. Aldebrand would be little help in battle at his best and after a day and a night in the clutches of the mystically animated fabric armour even less so.

"What do we do?" he asked.

"We?" she said, dismissively. "You stay right here. I have to free them."

"There are five of them. With swords and pistols," he observed, stroking Strelka's wing gently. "You have a broken sword and a knife."

"It is a shame I don't have wings," she said, thoughtfully.

"You might not, but I do," said the young Lord with more spine than she had imagined him capable of.

"And have you some better weapons in your pockets, perchance?" she asked, waggling her broken cutlass for emphasis.

He looked past her, eyeing the discarded fabric of the suit that had possessed him so recently. "In my pockets? No."

She followed his gaze and cuffed him lightly behind the ear with her empty left hand. "Don't be a fool. You just shed that damnable thing, at a hellish cost."

"Not me," he said, meeting her eyes.

For a moment, she could not make her mind grasp what he was suggesting. It was unthinkable and she wondered if she had misheard him. As she realized what he was suggesting, she froze. "What?" she cried hoarsely. The idea was so repulsive that it took all her self-control to hold down a shriek of horror at the notion.

She must keep her voice controlled, she knew. Her only advantage was that the brigands below did not know she was there, giving her the element of surprise. She calculated the advantage would likely fall short, but it was all she had.

"I recall little. The last day feels like a hazy dream that I watched another crawl through, but I do recall that the motivating force that possessed me was disappointed that though I carry the blood of its creators, I am no warrior. It craved battle and to share that battle with one who could share its appetite."

"And you think to feed it my soul?" she asked, aghast.

"I believe that I was not strong enough to control the power and thus the power overtook me. There is a chance that you might be of the right warrior spirit to wrestle it to heel and put it properly to use."

"And if I cannot?"

"The rogues who hold our comrades likely die either way. The only question is whether you can end the slaughter with their lives or if we all die here this night."

"With me roaming the pass as some possessed lich should I fail," Sonya added with a shudder.

"A possibility," he conceded with a shrug. "Unless you can whistle up a cannon and a new band of swords, I see no other options. Not ones that rescue our comrades, at least."

"We could simply leave them," Sonya said without conviction.

"I have known you but these past days, Red Sonya of Rogatino," he chided, "but I know you to be honourable. And far too dutiful to truly entertain that thought." He looked again over her shoulder and then into her eyes and added, "You could not live with that shame."

"I'll likely die of it," she replied dryly.

*****

Aldebrand gathered the cloth of the strange, mystical suit that had so recently been the cause of so much death and misery. Though it was his idea, he was loath to touch the thing at first. Once he raised his courage and grabbed hold of it, what he held felt like nothing more than an oddly heavy piece of canvas, albeit one that was a single garment that made up leggings and a sleeved tunic. There were no ties or buttons, simply a seam that opened from neck to crotch and then forked to the ankles of the strange suit. No sign of the damage Sonya's hand inflicted on it remained except that the now-dormant light panel had no cover.

The cover lay not far from where he had shed the skin of horror that had overtaken his mind and to their astonishment, when he mated the oval to the garment, it instantly reattached itself with a strange, metallic click and an oddly resonant hum. The panel beneath remained open and accessible.

"I do not recall how I came to be wearing this, but it appears that you simply shrug it on like a coat," he suggested.

Sonya eyed the innocent-looking tangle of cloth he held out to her, fighting her shudder down with effort. "A coat that may well rend my soul to shreds," she growled, covering her terror with a skin of anger. Throwing herself into battle with five mountain bandits with only a broken sword and a dagger was as nothing to finding the courage to don this alien and unnatural garment.

"Once you are ready, I will fly you down. I have never tried to carry another and my wings are not strong enough for a long flight at the best of times," he said, ignoring her hesitation. In truth, he was equally terrified, never having consciously struck another in anger, let alone taken up arms in a life-and-death battle.

"So I might don this foul tunic only to plummet to my death?" she asked, archly.

He nodded uncertainly.

"Should we survive this, let your future wife make the plans," she said, clapping him amiably on the shoulder. Her courage buoyed by the moment of levity, she snatched the suit from his grasp and twisted it around her like a death shroud.

Beneath her hands, the oddly heavy material at first felt like simple canvas, heavier than sailcloth, but with a similar tough, slightly rough texture. At first, it felt like wrapping a shawl over her shoulders, but then a slipping, greasy feeling overtook her as the cloth *moved* of its own volition. To her horror, it expanded and tightened simultaneously, a wisp of material wrapping around her face, stifling her scream as the seams sealed around her limbs and torso, taking on the shape of her like a second skin. Fighting down panic, she found that she could breathe normally, despite the film clinging to the planes of her face.

Before her, Aldebrand suddenly took on a glow and a flat, sexless voice sounded in her head, "***Stealth suit damaged, power minimal. Camouflage mode disabled.***"

Sonya's head whipped around, seeking the source of the voice but only Aldebrand stood nearby and the voice had not been his.

It continued, disturbingly conversationally, "***Greetings, Red Sonya of Rogatino. Instructions?***"

Sonya stared at the slightly glowing form of Aldebrand, numbly. When he had worn this suit, he had become a crazed and implacable engine of destruction. What she was experiencing did not seem to be taking her in anything like that direction. "Instructions?" she asked, finally.

"***The stealth suit awaits direction. Now that the power reserves have once again risen above survival minimums, some functions are available for selection,***" it explained.

Sonya struggled to comprehend what she was being told. "Functions?"

"***Basic functions are available for selection. Stealth is offline due to low power. Basic defense functions available. Basic and intermediate attack modes also available, though only for a limited duration.***"

"Why did you possess Aldebrand and kill my men?" she demanded.

"***Searching. Aldebrand. Tanaghaara descendant. Instructions unclear. Access to organic energy.***"

Sonya thought she understood. Her mind was uncomfortably full of images not her own, roots emerging from within, pulling life from anything within reach. She sensed unimaginable stretches of time where it dug into the soil around it with its fibrous tendrils to sap enough energy to keep itself alive.

After all that time, Aldebrand passed close enough to awaken it but it had been confused and he had been dreaming when it latched onto him, maybe sleepwalking, she realized. The whole attack had been the suit pulling energy from the men to sustain itself, likely with Aldebrand's dreaming mind directing the horror. The boy likely imagined himself in some dream the whole time.

"Attack mode?" she asked the air, intrigued.

"***Basic attack mode fully functional. Intermediate available, limited duration.***"

"My comrades are being held by at least five men and I have no powder for my pistols," she said, hoping the suit was what she now believed it to be.

"***Terrain?***" it asked.

"We are above, in cover."

"***Intermediate attack mode recommended. Internal weaponry available, limited power.***"

"Internal weaponry?"

"***Mono-molecular blade. Specify length, balance and hand preference.***"

"Mono...I know that..." She picked the dagger the Lady Raven had given her from the ground where she had laid it beside her broken cutlass hilt. "Like this?" she asked.

"***Tanagaara mono-molecular dagger, standard grip, balance for female musculature.***"

"And you can make a saber like this? Balanced for me?" she asked, hope rising.

"***Left or right-hand preference?***"

"Right," she said. The word had hardly left her lips when the comfortable, familiar weight of a deliciously balanced saber blossomed in her hand. The blade glowed slightly, but she assumed that was an effect of the clinging film over her eyes, similar to the way Aldebrand now glowed. She took an experimental swing at a low bush and watched in delight as the blade slipped effortlessly through several limbs as if they were made of gossamer. The very air seemed to part as she drew the blade through it.

Despite how wrong she knew it was, the horror that this thing had inflicted on her and those in her charge, and the evil that she could feel behind every stroke of the strange and exquisitely balanced blade, Sonya could feel herself accepting the clinging, cloying, living but not alive armour of the Tanaghaara. More, she felt it embrace her, hungrily.

"Aldebrand," she said with a grin, "get ready to fly."

CHAPTER 12

If climbing through the air with Lady Raven had been exhilarating, plummeting from the cliff with Aldebrand was anything but. Sonya had leapt from great heights many times in her life, often to escape death or deal it from above. She was familiar with the sensation of falling for long enough to register how dangerous what she was doing was. This was that awareness slowed only enough to add to the terror.

Aldebrand's stunted wings were barely enough to keep him aloft. With a Herculean effort, at the last moment he was able to slow their descent just enough that her landing atop the brigand nearest Sven was only incredibly painful rather than bone-shattering. The man beneath her did not fare as well.

Angling so the outside of her foot caught him at the base of the neck, he was dead before he hit the ground, his neck snapping with a muffled crack. Sonya rode his toppling form to the earth, rolling nimbly away from the corpse and instantly finding her feet when her momentum had bled away.

She turned to face the remaining bandits, knife in one hand and the magically provided saber gripped lightly in the other. She spun it once, experimentally and at once felt the perfection of the balance and the wrongness of the slithering, greasy feeling that the blade sent up her arm and into her soul.

"At last," she heard herself say, but the words were not her own.

The men in the canyon were stunned at the sudden appearance of a shadowed figure. Aldebrand had careened off, his wings flapping frantically as he tried to regain the safety of the heights. She had instructed him to leave the work ahead to her, his clumsy presence more likely to hinder her than be of any further assistance. Now there were only four, and Sonya had survived worse odds in her time.

Five.

Behind her, gravel crunched as the fifth man charged from the shadows. Perhaps he had been standing watch, perhaps simply relieving himself, but whatever turn of fate had hidden him from her until now, he did not hesitate to turn it to his immediate advantage.

She felt the impact of a sword strike slam down on her shoulder and was dumbfounded when only a dull, mildly painful impact registered. The blow should have cleaved her to her ribcage. Like her assailant, she did not waste the turn of fate that had spared her. She spun like a she-wolf, saber blade leading, low and savage. She let her momentum turn her a full circle, the assailant's body hardly slowing her blade as she drove the magical steel through skin, muscle, organs and bone. He was still alive when his body toppled off a pair of legs left standing by the swift and keen blade.

The four men facing her had not been idle. They closed the distance even as she drove her attack into the man at her back. When she again faced them, they had closed within a few sword lengths. The sight of their comrade sliced cleanly in two at the waist slowed their headlong rush and two of them drew up short, wrestling pistols from belt or sash. She stepped protectively between Sven and the nearest man as he levelled his flintlock at her chest.

These men were battle-hardened and saw a single woman as little threat. The pistol barked, the strange gossamer film over her face somehow blunting the blinding flash. She felt the ball impact her chest between her breasts, but the expected agony of the ripping, burning lead never came. She felt a thudding impact, as if punched by a woman. The magic of the magical skin had again protected her where no armour she could imagine would have.

"Now, we feast," she heard herself say. Neither the words nor the grin that split her features was entirely her own. She realized that she now fought two battles and could afford to lose neither, lest her comrades suffer the consequences.

With a leap that outdistanced any she had ever made, she pounced on the man with the now empty pistol. She batted it from his hand with her offhand, the short blade of her dagger drawing its point along the man's arm as she swung. The steel bit deep and opened his flesh from wrist to elbow, exposing bone. Blood fountained in a graceful arc from a severed artery, the brigand screaming as he clamped his other hand over the wound. The blade in her right hand slid through his soft belly, and with a twist, she ripped it free.

Three.

The suit that wore her drove her relentlessly back to the fray. The next nearest man was fumbling with his pistol, a fine-looking weapon that he had obviously stolen. He had forgotten to prime the pan and was desperately fumbling with his powder to finish the loading. Another impossible leap sent her slamming into him like a cannon shot. Her charge took him from his feet and her blade drank deeply as he fell. She wasn't certain if she or the strange, probing intelligence of the alien fabric had directed the blow.

Two.

The pistol spun up out of the man's dying hand and with a thought she didn't truly understand, she directed the magically provided sword to retract, leaving her right hand free to snatch the tumbling weapon from the air. She brought it up, aimed at the closest remaining bandit and fired. The weapon made a sad, pathetic 'whuff' and with a little puff of smoke, the lead ball dropped from the muzzle and clinked on the stones at her feet. A fine weapon, loaded by a fool. Her hand felt an odd catch on the metal above the trigger and a look confirmed her suspicion.

"Typical woman," grinned the man as he advanced on her. She could smell his rank odour from where she stood and his broken-toothed rictus grin made it clear what he intended once he closed the distance. Sonya still held the pistol as she had when it misfired, level with his eyes. He stalked closer, sword held loosely at his side, advancing on a woman with an empty pistol and a knife; he showed no concern.

He stopped just short of her, pressing his face deliberately, mockingly into the barrel of the fine, empty pistol, the hollow tube grinding against his cheek, just below the eye. "No balls," he said with an ugly, leering laugh.

Sonya's index finger caressed the hidden catch, releasing a spring loaded blade that ran the length of the barrel, artfully hidden by the fine filigree of inlaid gold and silver along the weapon's length. It drove through the cheek on a slight upward angle, the exquisitely sharp tip slicing into the man's brain.

"I do not need balls," she growled as the man slid lifeless from the wet steel to slump at her feet. "Idiot."

One.

The last brigand was smart enough to understand he was outmatched. Rather than join the battle, he had sprung to Lady Raven's side and cruelly hauled her to her feet by her broken wing. She muffled a shriek of pain and batted ineffectually at the man, but her strength was clearly sapped from her injury and he ignored her flailing arms if as if they were nothing. He poked his curved sword blade into the side of her neck, stilling her protests and drawing a tiny, perfect drop of blood that drew a thin line down her long, white throat. To her credit, she did not plead for her life or dissolve into tears. She merely glared at the man as best she could without turning her head and driving the blade deeper.

With a twist, he backed her away from Sonya, towards the mounts tethered across the narrow span of the pass.

Sonya tossed the pistol and its short blade into the shadows and called on the magic to rearm her with a saber. She followed the man, keeping pace and calling, "Get away from her, svolotsch!" as she leapt. Powered by the strange energy of the suit, the leap was beyond what any human should have managed, catching the man off guard. Her blade took his head from his shoulders, and a few metal feathers from the Lady Raven's helm sliced free in the stroke.

A cry of pleasure, hungry and sated at the same moment erupted from Sonya's lips as she landed, the sword again retracting into the magical fabric of the suit. Triumph!

But the exultation was not hers. Sonya revelled in battle, to be sure, but this was more. A deeper hunger that gnawed and slavered for more even as the last of her foe's blood seeped into the dirt at her feet. It was all she could do to hold the ravenous battle hunger at bay. Sven and even Lady Raven provoked the barely restrained violence simply by being close at hand. This thing wanted nothing but to end life and drink deeply of the energy within in a way that sickened Sonya to her core.

The Lady Raven reached up and grasped Sonya's wrist. Sonya intended to help the winged woman to her feet, but the suit pushed an unbidden impulse into her arm to twist away from the grip. The hand clamped down harder and the other hand joined it, fumbling at the oval cover on the inside of Sonya's forearm.

A deft twist, a ringing click and the little oval popped open. Lights danced and squirmed within. A mailed finger stabbed into the tiny aurora and suddenly Sonya was slumping to the ground, drained from the effort of fending off the slavering hunger of the enveloping fabric. Suddenly free, she gratefully collapsed to her knees.

EPILOGUE

Aldebrand climbed down from the cliff, his progress surprisingly nimble. His stubby wings seemed to balance him, and their beating kept him held hard against the rock face. Sonya wondered if his clumsiness was a result of the binding of his wings beneath the greatcoat he had worn most of their acquaintance.

When he reached them, Strelka sat on his shoulder, her talons drawing little beads of blood from the flesh beneath them. If he felt it, he gave no sign. A genuine smile warmed his features as he strode to Sonya's side as she worked the bindings on Sven's wrists open. She had tucked the strange knife given to her by the Lady Raven into the back of her belt once again. The discarded fabric of the suit lay in a heap and Aldebrand eyed it suspiciously and gave it a wide berth as he approached.

"Four men!" he exclaimed. "By the time I found a place to land and turned to watch, it was a thing already done!"

"Five," she corrected, pointing to the corpse hidden in shadow.

"I had intended to heave stones from the heights to aid the rescue," Aldebrand offered sheepishly, "but there was no need."

"That," she pointed to the slack mound of fabric, "did the killing. I only gave it form."

"You did not succumb," put in the Lady Raven. She was wrenching her broken wing around, the manipulation giving Sonya a queasy feeling as she watched her twist and set the bone. She did not have wings of her own for comparison, but if the broken bones of the lady's pinions felt pain as human flesh, the damage should have had her screaming in agony as she reset it.

"Does that not...pain you, Lady Raven?" Aldebrand asked, echoing Sonya's thoughts. He winced as an audible snap sounded from somewhere within the broken wing.

"Aye. The magic that aids my flight and grants me grander wings than yours dulls the agony, but it is," she grunted as she gave the offending bone a final, decisive twist that brought the wing back into symmetry with the other, "exquisitely painful all the same."

"Magic," said Sonya, suspicion flaring.

"Yes, Red Sonya of Rogatino," said the Lady. "My natural wings are much as Aldebrand's. Adequate for short flights and longer glides. Little more." She spread her magnificent plumes, pumping them gently, experimentally. She winced but did not cry out. "When a full-blooded Tanaghaara such as I is reborn, we are drawn to a magic that came to this world with us. We seek it instinctively and are drawn to it as a lodestone to the North Star."

Sonya had sailed aboard a vessel whose captain had possessed such a magical stone and been amazed to see it spin in a cup and align itself to the pole star no matter how the cup was manipulated.

"And this magic differs from *that* magic?" she demanded of the winged woman, jabbing an angry finger at the crumpled bundle of fabric. A trick of the light gave her to imagine movement in that pile, but when she looked closer, the innocent-looking heap of cloth did not so much as rustle in the light breeze that blew her scarlet tresses playfully around her head.

"Aye," said the Lady Raven, wearily. "My wings are wholly under my control, my people's magic simply adds to their size, strength and resilience. There is no mind at work but my own."

There was real enthusiasm in Aldebrand's voice as he hopefully asked, "And might I find this magic, Lady?"

Replacing her raven helm and giving it a firm twist to set it aright over her head and luscious black curls, she shook her now beaked head. "I fear not

Aldebrand. Were you meant to claim a share of that magic, you would have been drawn to it 'ere now. My vessel carried a receptacle that holds the magic fast for me in each incarnation. The man I hunt, the fugitive from my realm, must have a similar receptacle that functions for him in the same fashion. I have hunted him to ground in many lifetimes and always, his wings are those of a full-blood Tanaghaara."

Sonya thought she heard something other than the respect of the hunter for the prey in the lady's tone, but she eschewed comment. What might arise between even mortal foes in a hundred lifetimes, she wondered. That the only other of her race in this realm was also the man she was tasked with hunting could only cause them both to suffer a profound loneliness, she imagined.

Aldebrand looked disappointed and Sonya misliked the look that replaced that disappointment. The boy was too used to getting his way and the lady's matter of fact denial had turned him uglier than she had yet seen him. When he saw her scrutinizing his countenance, he wrestled his features to a more neutral and friendly mask in an instant.

"What will you do now, Red Sonya of Rogatino?" asked the Lady Raven.

"I would see Lord Aldebrand to his bride, as I was charged," she answered. "If Sven here is up to it, we will ride the last leagues before the day grows any older. I would quit these peaks," she finished with an unashamed shudder.

"Nothing would suit me finer," said Sven with a grin. He trotted off to saddle their mounts.

"And what of my return journey, Sonya?" asked Aldebrand, warily eyeing the heap of fabric as did Sonya.

"I will collect the stealth suit and see that its magic is properly contained," offered the Lady Raven. "It will not trouble you further, either of you."

Sonya could not argue that there was a better solution, though she would have preferred to know that the foul magic would be destroyed rather than contained. Somehow, she doubted that the Lady Raven would entertain that option.

"I have flint and steel," she suggested anyhow.

"The fabric is no simple cloth, as well you have both seen. No fire would touch it," explained the winged woman. Understanding their trepidation, she added, "I give you my word, the power will be contained. It is of my people and I know well the danger it poses and how it might be gentled."

"Then returning through the pass will be safe," said Aldebrand with something between relief and disbelief.

"Save the bandits, flash floods and rockfalls," reminded Sonya, dryly.

"And the mountain lions," added the lady with a grin.

"Ah," said the young lord. "Would you deign to serve as my escort on the return journey, Red Sonya of Rogatino?" he asked with a hopeful smile.

"I fear your noble father would not look upon my return with kindness. I still owe a debt for the death of that thrice-cursed lout in the tavern. I relish not years in indentured service."

"The notion of this woman in service to anyone makes me pity the one holding that lead," said the Lady Raven with a sincere chuckle.

Aldebrand looked back and forth between the two women and finally said, "If there are two women less suited to servitude, I should never like to meet them."

The two shared a look. Neither allowed their smiles to leave their eyes. Aldebrand ducked his head in mock submission when they turned their glares upon him.

"So where does Red Sonya of Rogatino look to set her feet once the young Lord is safely seen to his bride?" asked Sven, returning at the head of a train of horses, saddled and pawing the ground in anticipation.

"East." she said with a shrug. I travelled east when I was entangled in this..." She gestured at the dead men, Aldebrand, the winged lady and the bundle of accursed cloth that still lay untouched where she had shed it,

"...debacle."

"East?" asked Aldebrand.

"In a library in the sultanate where I had taken service as a sellsword, I read of an island in the ocean of Indus, rumoured to be ruled by fierce warrior women," Sonya said with a casual shrug. "I should like to see such a thing with my own eyes."

"Myth," scoffed Aldebrand. "I have read of such an isle and another much like it, somewhere off the coast of the Greco peninsula. No such storied and improbable race of women warriors walks this earth, in any ocean."

Sonya turned her gaze to the Lady Raven, resplendent in her elegant and superbly crafted armour, wings arched over her proud shoulders, raven helm perched precisely on her head. Her faintly glowing war club, studded with wicked spikes spun lazily from a thong wrapped around her wrist.

She returned Sonya's amused look with one of her own, taking in the other woman's blood- and dirt-spattered tunic, the worn leather gauntlets and high boots, a brace of pistols in her thick leather belt and the Lady's own gifted dagger tucked in the small of her back. She held no sword, her own snapped by Aldebrand when he had battled her under the thrall of the stealth-suit.

"I'm sure you're correct, young Aldebrand," conceded the Lady Raven. "A race of warrior women is too fantastic to credit."

"In any ocean," added Sonya, straight-faced.

The party rode out of the pass, single file. Behind them, the Lady Raven gathered the little bundle of fabric into a pouch, bound it tightly and with a mighty leap, took to the air. Sonya watched until the winged woman vanished from sight. As strange as the woman with the wings had been, as much strife as her presence had brought to this journey, she was sorry to see the last of her.

Aldebrand too watched the lady as she departed. His expression was thoughtful and calculating. He noted her direction carefully, as one who marked a path he might one day tread.

In the pass, a lone length of thread that had been sliced free of the alien fabric stirred...and hungrily burrowed into the rocky soil.

Seeking.

HOUSE OF CROM

THE GAUNTLET OF NABU

A SOLOMON KANE TRACT

JAMES L. RICHARDSON

HOUSE OF CROM

THE GAUNTLET OF NABU

A SOLOMON KANE TRACT

JAMES L. RICHARDSON

CHAPTER 1

"By damn!" said Josiah Campbell as his plow snagged on yet another stone hidden beneath the soil. Sara would have his hide for the curse, but this morning was the very earth was fighting him for every inch. If they were going to make it through another winter, this acreage would need to be fruitful and multiply the seed in his satchel into a bountiful crop of turnips.

At the rate that he was going this morning, he might gather enough stones to rebuild the chimney, but they would have nothing to cook in the hearth come Easter Sunday. This new land might be what the good Lord promised the meek, but there was no mercy in it. There was precious little left in the root cellar from last year's gleanings, but at the least he might expect a hot, if painfully thin soup for his supper this eventide now that Sarah had finally risen from her maternity bed.

The babe seemed hale, if not entirely hearty. They had settled on calling him Samuel after Sarah's brother. At least he quieted when he took the teat, though Sarah sobbed in those moments to fill the silence.

The field might stubbornly resist his efforts to sow their survival, but it was blessedly quiet, he thought with a guilty smile.

The stone must be freed from the earth so he angrily snatched up his shovel and set to the task. A few minutes work had the top of the stone exposed. Only it was too smooth, too regular to be a stone. The local tribes were migratory, so it wasn't likely to be one of their pagan burials. He could not think what else it might be. It was taking up too much of his day, but the field was small and each portion had value, leaving him little choice but to dig deeper. At least the dark, rich soil would be easy to till once he filled the hole back in.

Smooth to the touch, when Josiah wiped the dirt from the orb, he was shocked to see the glow of gold revealed by the sweaty rag he used to scrub the surface. Surely it must be brass. Who would bury gold in a field in this untamed land? He had been told that the native tribes did not value suchlike as civilized folk did, so who could have come this way and left such a treasure in his field?

A name came unbidden into his mind. A word he did not know from a voice he could not hear.

Nabu.

The more he cleaned the dirt from the surface, the more strangeness was revealed. He mouthed furious prayers as writing such as he had never seen, swirls and strange looping script intersected with inset shapes that gave him a cold, queasy feeling when he tried to make sense of them. The harder he looked the more it felt like the writing was moving beneath his gaze, twisting and writhing as if it did not wish to be looked upon. He could almost feel the graven images squirming under his fingers, the slick surface trying to slide free of his grasp.

And there was heat. Unnaturally, the orb felt warm and alive in his hands. As he knelt in the loose dirt of the hole he had carved into the field, the cold of the earth seeped into his bones through the wet fabric of his breeches. The chill air fogged his breath, the spring breeze biting through his thin tunic and he could hardly feel his toes, the wrappings inside his boots soaked through from the morning's trudge through the frosty grass.

Yet his hands and even his arms were warm, almost to the point of pain.

In his head, a different alien name thundered, eclipsing the first, growing louder as the heat of the orb grew. A name he had never in his life heard singing in his ears now felt like the welcoming embrace of his darling Sarah. The caress of the name was as the rare moments when love and duty met, those times in the deep of winter when the fire had begun to die and she needed his manly warmth to fill her womanhood.

"Anzu," he whispered, the fog of his breath carrying the name across the field.

CHAPTER 02

Evil. This land was soaked in it and Solomon Kane could feel it, the way an old soldier felt a winter storm in the wind as it chilled the musket balls still lodged beneath battle-scarred skin. The dark, writhing sins that lodged in Kane's soul felt the evil in the wind as it slipped through the pines and down the trail toward him. As ever, he could no more escape its pull than bring back all that the Dark One had already taken from him.

The church was tiny, its lichyard overgrown and unkempt. Several markers had toppled, and what headstones still stood were half-buried in leaves that obscured the crudely carved names and dates. For all its sad neglect, the evil that drew Kane onward slid around this little building and its crooked stones as a stream 'round a boulder. He would give a great deal to feel that sort of soft, untidy tranquility within his regimented soul.

Perhaps a younger man might tend the yard with more vigour, but the stooped old man wore his piety like a cloak. Even his feeble strokes with his reed broom showed a love and reverence that Kane could not help but admire. Sunlight streamed across the single room of the little church, dust motes dancing cheerily in the beams. "Have you the time to give blessing to a weary traveller, good father?" he called from the doorway.

"The Lord has guided you to my humble hall, good traveller. We are but servants to His plan," answered the priest with a cough. "Though, your younger legs might carry you the last few yards to my altar and save these old bones the journey."

Doffing his hat and bowing his head in supplication as he crossed the threshold, Kane's well-muscled form seemed to fill the tiny church as he entered. He dwarfed the bent priest, his eyes almost level with the elder as he dropped to his knees to take the blessing. The paper-thin skin of the old man's hands fairly glowed as he raised them above Kane's bowed head, the light streaming from the window above almost outlining the bones beneath the flesh. Unconsciously, he moved his hands as far as he could from the pistols and the rapier in his belt.

The blessing complete, Kane stood, and the priest squinted up at him. "You are no simple traveller, my son," he pronounced with certainty.

"God sets me to where my skills can be of use," said Kane.

"And so He does." A rattling cough shook the old man and he wiped spittle from his beard with a cloth he plucked from his sleeve. "Something troubles this land and I believe the Lord has sent a troubled soul in search of redemption. By your weapons and your bearing, you are no stranger to righteous battle."

"The Lord directs my blade and my aim," intoned Kane, his gaze far away, "but there is little of righteousness in the plying of my trade."

"Each man carries the burden the Lord fashions for him. That burden may bow your back, but the Lord gives unto men such as you the thews to carry it still," pronounced the priest, sadly. He reached up and placed a hand on Kane's shoulder and gave it a gentle squeeze.

"Your trouble, priest?" demanded Kane, shrugging off the sympathy and the hand.

"The Campbell homestead has come 'neath the gaze of evil," explained the old man, again coughing up something unspeakable from the depths of his chest. "If Christ intends that you grapple with demonic forces, your path lies in that direction."

"Show me," Kane demanded.

CHAPTER 03

Sarah Campbell was still recovering from the effects of a difficult pregnancy and recent childbirth. Pain showed in her every action as she bustled around the small room that served as kitchen, parlour and bedchamber. The crude stone chimney leaked smoke into the room, a fine layer of soot settling on every surface. Solomon Kane could taste it in the weak brew of mint leaves she had offered him, shamefaced at the lack of better.

He sipped politely, and bade her recount the whole tale. As he had expected from what the priest had told him, there was indeed a taint of elder evil in her words. It hung about the little cabin, greasily coating every surface as palpably as the unwelcome soot from the hearth.

Despite her obvious panic over events of recent days, Kane was impressed with the woman's recollection of detail. The descriptions she gave of the strange writing on the pendant that she believed had taken the soul of her husband drew images in his mind and he knew that the pendant she spoke of was indeed a relic of ancient magic. How it had come to this new world and been buried in an anonymous pasture in the Province of Massachusetts Bay was a mystery he could not fathom, but here it had lain and Josiah Campbell had disturbed that eldritch power and mayhap paid an unimaginable price for it.

"Josiah set it right there," said Sarah Campbell, pointing to the centre of the only table in her tiny cabin. Kane sat on one of her two chairs, she paced ceaselessly, eschewing the other. "It called to him, he kept saying," she added with a sharp sob.

"Over a fortnight, you say?" he asked, shifting his weight to settle his sword-belt more comfortably. The rickety chair creaked alarmingly 'neath his weight as he twisted his muscular form. "He was himself in those first days?"

"Aye, good sir. He rose before dawn, plowed and sowed, returned at dusk for eventide's meal. He would sit there," she stabbed at the empty chair, "by candlelight for hours afterwards though, only staring and muttering." She shook her head and hid her eyes as she added, "Tending the babe kept me from paying much attention. He's powerful vexed with the colic."

Kane nodded his understanding and said nothing, encouraging her to continue.

"Truth be told, I was grateful that something took his attention from...me." She could not meet his eyes but after a deep breath, she added, "I am a dutiful wife, but only newly risen from the maternity bed. The babe and the hearth tax the limits of my recovering strength."

Looking around, Solomon saw the empty cradle, crudely carved from greenwood, but no sign of the child. "And this past night, you say he was overtaken by something...evil," he said, searching her red-rimmed and puffy eyes. "When the moon turned new, your husband..."

"Josiah," she said flatly. "He was agitated and restless through the night. I thought he might..." she turned away, colouring. "When I awoke this morning, Josiah was gone." She pointed at the vacant cradle and sobbed deeply, "He took Samuel!"

Alone, with no chaperone, Kane could not offer even a comforting hand to this good wife. He was uncomfortable with so much female emotion and rose from the table, setting his clay cup to rocking in his haste. "I take my leave, good wife Campbell. This evil must be brought to heel and the sun is still high. If your husband and child yet live, perhaps there is hope. The Lord will not fail you."

"I can do naught but pray, good sir Kane. I shall add your name to my invocations this day."

Without another word, Solomon Kane spun on a heel and strode from the tiny cottage. The trail left by Josiah Campbell had been apparent even as he strode up to the door earlier in the day. The man had blundered into the woods on a night with no moon and the evidence of his passage was as clear as if he had unspooled a skein of wool behind him.

The only question was if Solomon Kane might run the fiend to ground before nightfall. From painful experience, Kane knew that any evil spell or sacrifice that was to be wrought using the pure, innocent blood of the infant would not begin while the sun still showed its face. Malevolence craved the dark.

Solomon Kane craved it as well.

CHAPTER 04

The trail wound without true purpose through the wood. Kane followed it with ease; broken branches, turned stones, scuffs in the moss all obvious signs, plain in the light of day. The longer he tracked, the more concern crowded his mind. An entity of the sort he believed was in play here usually had a more certain agenda and would flee unerringly to whatever place of power it sought for its dark purpose. This trail spoke of panic and confusion, not intent.

Near dusk, Kane spied movement ahead and sounds came to him not of the wood but of his quarry forcing a way through it. Cursing, crashing, snapping sounds, punctuated with a sharply hushed cry of an infant. He was close.

Kane read the curve of the land around him and cut a path to his right, running hard and low, staying silent. The man he tracked was making enough noise that he hardly need take great caution to mask his progress, but the habits of a lifetime wrote the poetry of his passage. Tracking his trail would take another with skill to match his own and no man would hear the sounds of his movements, for he made none.

Josiah Campbell stumbled into a twilit glade, boughs reaching and snagging his torn tunic, limbs whipping his unprotected face cruelly as he shielded the babe from their sting with both arms. He stopped short, his ragged boots digging little furrows in the soft earth as he skidded to a halt. A man in a tall, buckled hat, crisp white linen blouse laced loosely at the throat under a black waistcoat that matched his tight black trousers sat casually on a mossy boulder in the clearing, wiping his tall black leather boots with a rag. He eyed the man and babe emerging from the wood with calm but measured eyes. His rapier was still in its sheath but something in his bearing told Josiah that the weapon could spring to hand viper quick and thrice as deadly, should the need arise.

"Your good wife fears for your soul, Josiah Campbell," intoned the stranger. "And the babe as well."

Though the stranger was seated, making it difficult to judge his true stature, Josiah was instantly aware that in a martial contest, he could stand no chance. He had the child to protect and was unarmed and unskilled at such things in any case. This powerful man had his rapier and likely a brace of pistols behind his belt. Still, if Sarah had sent him, there was no choice.

"Stand aside, stranger. My son is my concern," he said with more conviction than he felt. Samuel gurgled and struggled in his arms. Josiah drew him closer, protectively.

The stranger's eyes narrowed, watching the pair.

"Your good wife would see the babe safe, as would I." said Solomon Kane. "I do not know what evil holds the reigns, but I do not see death in your eyes. Mayhap we take the child to the church where all might be certain of the Lord's protection," he suggested, his tone casual but his eyes wary.

Campbell looked slowly around the glade, a man clearing his mind of fog. He narrowed his eyes in concern. He had been running so long he had left behind the part of the forest he knew and sudden realization dawned that even if he wanted to, he likely could not find his way home from here. As the light faded, he would have no shelter, no fire, no food or milk for the child. Death stalked these woods in a hundred forms and he had stumbled into them blindly. Fool!

Yet if this stranger had tracked him at Sarah's behest, the man was no friend.

As if reading his thoughts, the stranger lifted a hand and pointed off to Josiah's right and said, "The Lord's house lies a few hours trek that way. Your flight has taken you in something of a circle, Master Campbell."

"A circle?" asked Josiah, horrified. He had been so certain he had cut a line away from the cottage. He had to get the child as far from the danger as he could and if he had somehow turned back toward home, the boy was in mortal danger. As was he.

"By the words of the old priest, I broke my journey to bespeak your good wife. I feared that some foul denizen of the pit had taken your soul. You show none of the signs and no innocent babe could cleave so close to one in evil's thrall without wailing in terror." He gestured with his chin at the child nuzzling contentedly at one of Josiah's dangling fingers. "There is more in this tale than I have been told. We can untangle the skein in the sanctuary of sacred ground."

The words were spoken quietly, almost reverently, but the steel look in the flint grey eyes backed them with a subtle but unmistakable threat.

"What is your name, stranger?" asked Josiah.

"I am called Solomon Kane," answered the man, sliding down off the boulder and giving Campbell a glimpse of his massive, muscular form. Armed or no, Josiah could not hope to match this Solomon Kane in any sort of combat. Every movement was coiled menace, every breath a warning.

"And what is my soul and that of my son to you, Solomon Kane?" asked Campbell, mustering his bravado.

"I am but a humble servant of Christ, treading a path set by the Lord. More often than I care to recall, that path puts me between innocent souls and servants of the Dark One," said Kane with resignation. "As you serve the life and soul of your boy, I serve those imperilled souls placed in my path."

"A pretty piece of oratory," said Campbell, skeptically. "If that be true, you won't mind taking the lead," he added with a wave of his hand in the direction Kane had indicated lay the questionable safety of the little church.

CHAPTER 05

Night fell like an axe blade and Kane had to slow his pace to allow Campbell to keep up with him in the feeble starlight. Kane noted that though he took constant wounds from branches snagging his clothing or slapping at his face, none so much as touched the child in his arms. When he stumbled, a desperate twist had landed him hard on his back, the babe safe atop him.

There was nothing of evil in the man that Kane could detect. And he could detect much.

There was a false witness and no mistake. Lies, the language of the damned, had drawn him into this evil. Kane would teach a fearsome lesson, or give his life in the effort. As ever, he could do no less.

His keen senses drew his attention to his right, the direction of the little cottage of the Campbells. Before he could swing back and face the danger, a cry told him he was too late. A crash of brush and the sudden infant wail in the gloom confirmed the suspicion he had formed as they had grown closer to the tiny church and its untidy lich yard.

The evil was not within the husband.

A horrid, palpitating cackle ripped though the trees, clasping an icy fist ’round Kane’s heart. Turning, he saw Josiah crumpled on the ground, alive but one arm torn off at the elbow, blood arcing into the air from the stump. Kane whipped a leather lace from the collar of his blouse and whipped it around the stump, staunching the arterial blood as best he could.

“You must rouse the priest, Josiah!” shouted Kane into the shocked face of the young farmer. With the thong tight around the bleeding stump, he shook the man with both hands. When that bore no fruit, a hard backhand slap and then another finally brought a soul searing wail of torment from the man. After it passed, Kane snapped a hand under the man's jaw, forcing his eyes to meet Kane's. "You will rouse the priest, Campbell." He pointed vigourously in the direction of the little church and again shook the man. "That direction, swift as you may. Loose your way and look to the middle star of Orion for direction. This time of year, it hangs over the church and you may rely on it if your other senses fail." Solomon squeezed the man's oozing stump for emphasis, to make certain he had his attention. "If you wish your child to live, you will rouse the priest and hie yourselves to your cottage by midnight!" Shoving the man to his feet, he pushed him in the required direction with an added, "GO!" for emphasis.

Campbell stopped and turned back to Kane. Clutching his bloody stump, he locked eyes with the taller man. "There was a vessel."

"And the amulet was within," concluded Kane. "I have seen suchlike before. A golden vase or cask, replete with mystical runes and symbols, no doubt."

Campbell nodded once. "I plucked it from the earth, but when it called to me in a voice I could not hear, I buried it again."

"You told Sarah of the gold," said Kane, certain he could see the shape of the thing, "but not the voice."

"She coveted the treasure. While I slept, she dug it up by moonlight and set it on our table by dawn. When I woke, she was already lost to it. She ignored the babe, the hearth-fire, even her own bodily needs for days."

"And then one night, she prized open the golden orb, revealing a pendant on a chain held within. Fashioned of blue-tinged gold, its heart a gem bright as a summer sky and as painful to look upon as the sun. The name Anzu again pounded in my head, but the call was louder still for Sarah," he continued. Kane wanted to scream at him to run to the church, but the tale continued to spill from the man unabated. In the distance a cry that might have been the babe cut weakly through the night air.

"There is little time, Master Campbell," ordered Kane with a steely glare.

"She placed the thrice-bedamned thing over her head, and my Sarah was gone. I am ashamed to say that I did not at first realize. For many nights, it was the bliss of our first days, Sarah loving as she hadn't since before we took ship for this new world," finished Josiah in a shamefaced rush.

"A tale of evil and no doubt, good Josiah," said Kane with impatience but not without sympathy. "I shall hear it in its full shape another time. Hie now for the priest. If there is to be any hope for your son, I need the priest to bring his secret tomes to your cottage. I do not know if I can wrestle this demon from your good wife, but if I can, his secret knowledge will be needed."

"Secret...knowledge?" asked Josiah, greatly puzzled.

"You do not need to know more, friend Campbell. You do not *want* to know more, friend," intoned Kane gravely. "True agents of the Lord hold greater responsibility than Sunday allegory and burying the dead," he finished cryptically.

Again, he pointed and ordered, "GO!"

CHAPTER 06

Kane's keen eyes picked out the trail left by the entity now wearing Sarah Campbell's skin. Even in the feeble starlight, it took little skill to track such a blundering, arrow straight course. He knew where the thing was heading in any case. The cottage.

In Kane's experience, such evil as this, contained for unknowable time by unfathomable power, would have but one goal: Destroy that power so that it could never again hold them in check.

The child's life would be the key to breaking such power. It was no coincidence that this evil had latched onto the mother of a newborn. The innocence of a babe was as ambrosia to the Dark One, conferring power when such innocence was channelled by sacrifice, an echo of the covenant of Abraham, twisted and befouled.

There was little time in hand and Kane left his own blundering trail in his desperate haste. This Anzu was lending mystical strength and speed to the Campbell woman's steps and he feared he might not arrive in time. Solomon Kane feared nothing in life for himself, but terror of what could befall the infant both in body and soul drove his mighty limbs to speed and power beyond any he had ever achieved. His heart bid fair to leap free from his chest, his breath coming in whooping gulps as he pounded through the pitch dark forest, branches and saplings snapping before him as he thundered relentlessly back to the Campbell home.

Kane's momentum drove him through the crude planks that served as the door to the cottage. Splinters and shards of wood exploded inward, across the room, some clattering into the fire that burned weakly in the hearth. On the table, the infant Samuel lay on his back, tiny fists and feet pumping furiously in the air above him, bellowing and bawling in cold fear. The shape of his mother loomed above him terribly, no hint of maternal kindness in the rictus that leered hungrily down on the child.

Around her neck, a chain of gold with a strange azure cast hung with a pendant of the same oddly tinted gold, a stone of cold, fire-kissed blue that seared his eyes to gaze upon set within. Whorled scrawls of a language Kane did not recognize writhed and twisted in the metal around the stone, snakes of language and horror curling and speaking without sound.

Upon the table, set at little Samuel's head, an urn of the strange blued gold sat empty, its lid set beside it. Mystic symbols also moved upon its surface. In a fashion he could not comprehend, that moving scroll of words he could not fathom drew his gaze as the pendant repulsed it. The little urn glowed faintly, yet as he watched, that glow dimmed as a voice sounded within the humble cabin.

No human voice, no mouth of flesh and bone could form the sounds that vomited forth from Sarah Campbell in that moment. The words, if words they were, drew trickles of blood from Solomon Kane's ears and unbidden icy tears from his eyes. The terrible sound beyond sound carried only one word that he could comprehend: Anzu.

Tearing his rapier from its scabbard, he leapt across the room, ignoring the cacophony that poured from Sarah's corrupted throat. He cut at her long, vulnerable neck, intent on severing her head from her body at a stroke. Impossibly, when the blow landed, the blade precisely impacted the thin gold chain and stopped as if Kane had aimed the blow at a granite wall. The reverberation of the strike bid fair to rip the hilt from his powerful grip.

One weapon useless, he ripped one of his pistols from his wide belt and in a blink, levelled and fired. His aim, as ever was true. The ball flew straight but instead of yielding flesh, the lead flattened harmlessly on the cold blue stone, the pendant inexplicably swinging into the bullet's path.

For a moment, the drumming, pounding thunder of Sarah's demonic voice became a menacing, mocking cackle of amusement before returning to the intoning of its foul and incomprehensible spell. Sarah's left hand, clenched into a claw raised above her head. As he watched, transfixed, the ragged, broken nails lengthened, pulling each into a fearsome, dagger point, their pink white tips shifting into a strange gold metallic material, tinted oddly with an unearthly blue.

The infant was lost. No weapon, no power in him was sufficient to stop this fiend. The evil would not be contained.

Contained.

A lunge brought him to the table, but his mighty thews could not bring his hands to the babe. Without a thought, he reached, not for the child, but for what sat just beyond his tiny head. The urn.

A fingertip brushed the strangely warm metal and without warning, Solomon Kane found himself...nowhere. No walls, no ceiling, no floor...yet he did not fall. He whipped his head around but there was simply nothing in every direction.

And then there was a voice.

Nabu.

CHAPTER 07

"Solomon Kane," intoned the voice, warm and commanding at once. "You must be my vessel. Anzu must not be loosed upon the world again."

Though the voice could only be divine, Kane could not contain his cynicism. "Does the Lord God command me?" he asked, surprised at the derision in his voice.

"I am Nabu, God of Word, Art and Wisdom. I was of Babylon before your Christ."

"I am the Lord, Thy God and thou shalt have no other gods before me," recited Kane. "That is the First Commandment."

"That you have none before Him does not preclude our existence, Solomon Kane. You have encountered elder gods before and will again. We do not require your worship, but occasionally, we do require your service."

"And if I will not serve a pagan 'god'?" he demanded.

"Then Anzu will sacrifice the child, destroying the vessel of Nabu, the only force which can contain his evil and chaotic essence, loosing his influence once again into the world," answered the disembodied voice. "Anzu once stole the Tablets of Destiny, hoping to unleash chaos. Had they not been recovered, mankind would have torn itself asunder before your kind even built the first fire in the first cave. Should he escape now, the bloodshed and death would be incalculable."

"Serving you would mean defying my Lord's commandment. You ask me to damn my soul for eternity," suggested Kane.

"The soul you bear is older than you imagine, Solomon Kane. It was old when the waters drank Atlantis, and it will inhabit countless warriors yet before it is touched by eternity."

There was a long silence. Kane felt the truth of it, heavy and cold as the grave.

"Your damnation," said the voice at last, "is this life, this battle, this moment." A sound that might have been a chuckle followed. "Your redemption as well."

"I believe you may be a god after all," said Kane.

"And what has changed your mind?"

"You speak a great deal, yet say nothing."

This time, there was no mistaking the deep, sonorous laugh.

And then, Solomon Kane was once again reaching across a rough plank table, his fingertip brushing the strangely warm metal of the urn. The metal touched him back.

It melted and slumped, flowing up his fingertip, encasing first that finger and then with a gentle, warm flow it enveloped the rest of his hand. In a trice, his hand was clad a golden gauntlet, the gold oddly tinted with a bluish hue and the whole metal glove covered in mystic, moving runes he could hear singing resonantly in his head.

On the other side of the table, her hand still poised to rip the infant between them to shreds, the thing that was Anzu screamed in rage, Sarah Campbell's mouth tearing impossibly wide in its fury.

And fear.

Of all the lessons his strange adventures had taught him, the most important was also the simplest. Hesitation was death.

Viper quick, the gauntleted hand whipped out, whatever mystical evil holding him immobile overcome by the countering power of Nabu. He snatched the pendant at Anzu's throat and ripped it from the chain in a single, fluid motion. The scream that erupted from Sarah Campbell's mouth was mercifully, wholly human.

A cold that tore the stones from the hearth tore through the cabin, Anzu's essence trying desperately to pull itself free of Kane's powerful grasp, the magic of the gauntlet wrestling desperately to contain the writhing, greasy demonic force pulsating within the cold, fiery blue stone. Even with the vast, immeasurable power of the spells within and upon the gauntlet, Kane felt his strength waning and in another moment, Anzu would break his hold.

A voice suddenly rang clear and firm from the shattered threshold of the cottage. Latin phrases that no church parishioner had ever heard shouted from a pulpit, echoed and pounded through the room, shattering loose hearthstones with their power. Anzu screamed without a voice.

The priest read from a small, leather bound tome. Kane recognized the ritual and hoped the old man had the strength for it. Though short and uncomplicated in its prayer, invoking this particular sacred rite was as dangerous and taxing for the priest as the evil it hoped to dispel was for Sarah Campbell.

Kane snatched the tiny, mewling babe from the table with his free hand. He did not dare release his grasp on the pendant, but Sarah had begun to flail and spasm in the grip of the ritual and he feared she might unknowingly strike the child a death blow in the battle for her immortal soul.

Josiah, his severed arm bound in a neat bandage and his face pale but set with determination, squeezed past the preacher. Avoiding the flailing limbs and swirling damnation, he ducked under Kane's arm and plucked Samuel from his grasp. His hand free, Solomon reached out and slammed Sarah's flailing form down onto the rough planked table in an attempt to keep her from injuring herself in her convulsions.

The ritual had but one last stanza to complete the prayer. The priest began the phrase and was suddenly taken with a fit of coughing, interrupting the prayer and allowing Anzu a resurgence. Kane threw his entire weight into holding Sarah down as the energy spewing from the amulet in his fist twisted and squirmed.

"Finish the invocation, priest!" he demanded.

With a final violent cough, the old man again intoned his ritual Latin, the power battering the essence of Anzu back and back again. The gauntlet took on a life beyond his hand and Kane stared in awe as the gauntlet again flowed and melted, this time enveloping the pendant in his fist in a vessel that completely enclosed the gold and stone within.

Kane, the priest and Josiah gaped at the golden skull in Kane's hand, its glow slightly glossed with an unnatural blue. Sarah moaned weakly from beneath Kane's restraining hand. For a moment, the universe was still.

With a contented gurgle, Samuel broke wind, wetly and loudly.

EPILOGUE

High in the hills, Solomon Kane tossed a satchel into the man-deep pit he had dug from the hard soil. Simply climbing to this place had taxed his great strength to near its limit. His hope was that by choosing this difficult to access cleft in these remote hills, no one would stumble across the relic he had buried as deeply as he could manage.

The golden skull of Nabu did not speak to him or change its form while he trekked the few days it took to find this isolated spot. He knew how evil called, and he meant to take the thrice-bedamned skull far beyond the reach of Sarah Campbell or her son. Anzu might be gentled and contained by the magic of Nabu, but that was no surety against its call someday leeching out again. The Campbells had suffered enough for a single lifetime and he would see them live and die without further eldritch evil interference in their lives.

As he hiked down the far side of the range, he looked back up the way he had come. For just a moment, he saw the ghostly form of a crenellated stone tower rising from the cleft in the hills where he had buried the golden skull of Nabu. A laugh rolled through the hills like thunder and when it passed, the vision of the tower, too, had vanished.

END

The Shadow of the Vulture

By Robert E. Howard

Originally Published in Magic Carpet Magazine, January 1934

The Magic Carpet Magazine, January 1934

CHAPTER 1

SO THEY BROUGHT the envoys, pallid from months of imprisonment, before the canopied throne of Suleyman the Magnificent, Sultan of Turkey, and the mightiest monarch in an age of mighty monarchs. Under the great purple dome of the royal chamber gleamed the throne before which the world trembled— gold-paneled, pearl-inlaid. An emperor's wealth in gems was sewn into the silken canopy from which depended a shimmering string of pearls ending a frieze of emeralds which hung like a halo of glory above Suleyman's head. Yet the splendor of the throne was paled by the glitter of the figure upon it, bedecked in jewels, the aigrette feather rising above the diamonded white turban. About the throne stood his nine viziers, in attitudes of humility, and warriors of the imperial bodyguard ranged the dais—Solaks in armor, black and white and scarlet plumes nodding above the gilded helmets.

The envoys from Austria were properly impressed—the more so as they had had nine weary months for reflection in the grim Castle of the Seven Towers that overlooks the Sea of Marmora. The head of the embassy choked down his choler and cloaked his resentment in a semblance of submission—a strange cloak on the shoulders of Habordansky, general of Ferdinand, Archduke of Austria. His rugged head bristled incongruously from the flaming silk robes presented him by the contemptuous Sultan, as he was brought before the throne, his arms gripped fast by stalwart Janizaries. Thus were foreign envoys presented to the sultans, ever since that red day by Kossova when Milosh Kabilovitch, knight of slaughtered Serbia, had slain the conqueror Murad with a hidden dagger.

The Grand Turk regarded Habordansky with scant favor. Suleyman was a tall, slender man, with a thin down-curving nose and a thin straight mouth, the resolution of which his drooping mustachios did not soften. His narrow outward-curving chin was shaven. The only suggestion of weakness was in the slender, remarkably long neck, but that suggestion was belied by the hard lines of the slender figure, the glitter of the dark eyes.

There was more than a suggestion of the Tatar about him—rightly so, since he was no more the son of Selim the Grim, than of Hafsza Khatun, princess of Crimea. Born to the purple, heir to the mightiest military power in the world, he was crested with authority and cloaked in pride that recognized no peer beneath the gods.

Under his eagle gaze old Habordansky bent his head to hide the sullen rage in his eyes. Nine months before, the general had come to Stamboul representing his master, the Archduke, with proposals for truce and the disposition of the iron crown of Hungary, torn from the dead king Louis' head on the bloody field of Mohacz, where the Grand Turk's armies opened the road to Europe.

There had been another emissary before him—Jerome Lasczky, the Polish count palatine. Habordansky, with the bluntness of his breed, had claimed the Hungarian crown for his master, rousing Suleyman's ire. Lasczky had, like a suppliant, asked on his bended knees that crown for his countrymen at Mohacz.

To Lasczky had been given honor, gold and promises of patronage, for which he had paid with pledges abhorrent even to his avaricious soul— selling his ally's subjects into slavery, and opening the road through the subject territory to the very heart of Christendom.

All this was made known to Habordansky, frothing with fury in the prison to which the arrogant resentment of the Sultan had assigned him. Now Suleyman looked contemptuously at the staunch old general, and dispensed with the usual formality of speaking through the mouthpiece of the Grand Vizier. A royal Turk would not deign to admit knowledge of any Frankish tongue, but Habordansky understood Turki. The Sultan's remarks were brief and without preamble.

"Say to your master that I now make ready to visit him in his own lands, and that if he fails to meet me at Mohacz or at Pesth, I will meet him beneath the walls of Vienna."

Habordansky bowed, not trusting himself to speak. At a scornful wave of the imperial hand, an officer of the court came forward and bestowed upon the general a small gilded bag containing two hundred ducats. Each member of his retinue, waiting patiently at the other end of the chamber, under the spears of the Janizaries, was likewise so guerdoned.

Habordansky mumbled thanks, his knotty hands clenched about the gift with unnecessary vigor. The Sultan grinned thinly, well aware that the ambassador would have hurled the coins into his face, had he dared. He half-lifted his hand, in token of dismissal, then paused, his eyes resting on the group of men who composed the general's suite— or rather, on one of these men. This man was the tallest in the room, strongly built, wearing his Turkish gift-garments clumsily. At a gesture from the Sultan he was brought forward in the grasp of the soldiers. Suleyman stared at him narrowly. The Turkish vest and voluminous khalat could not conceal the lines of massive strength. His tawny hair was close-cropped, his sweeping yellow mustaches drooping below a stubborn chin. His blue eyes seemed strangely clouded; it was as if the man slept on his feet, with his eyes open.

"Do you speak Turki?" The Sultan did the fellow the stupendous honor of addressing him directly. Through all the pomp of the Ottoman court there remained in the Sultan some of the simplicity of Tatar ancestors.

"Yes, your majesty," answered the Frank.

"Who are you?"

"Men name me Gottfried von Kalmbach."

Suleyman scowled and unconsciously his fingers wandered to his shoulder, where, under his silken robes, he could feel the outlines of an old scar.

"I do not forget faces. Somewhere I have seen yours—under circumstances that etched it into the back of my mind. But I am unable to recall those circumstances."

"I was at Rhodes," offered the German.

"Many men were at Rhodes," snapped Suleyman.

"Aye." agreed von Kalmbach tranquilly. "De l'Isle Adam was there."

Suleyman stiffened and his eyes glittered at the name of the Grand Master of the Knights of Saint John, whose desperate defense of Rhodes had cost the Turk sixty thousand men. He decided, however, that the Frank was not clever enough for the remark to carry any subtle thrust, and dismissed the embassy with a wave.

The envoys were backed out of the Presence and the incident was closed. The Franks would be escorted out of Stamboul, and to the nearest boundaries of the empire. The Turk's warning would be carried posthaste to the Archduke, and soon on the heels of that warning would come the armies of the Sublime Porte.

Suleyman's officers knew that the Grand Turk had more in mind than merely establishing his puppet Zapolya on the conquered Hungarian throne. Suleyman's ambitions embraced all Europe—that stubborn Frankistan which had for centuries sporadically poured forth hordes chanting and pillaging into the East, whose illogical and wayward peoples had again and again seemed ripe for Moslem conquest, yet who had always emerged, if not victorious, at least unconquered.

It was the evening of the morning on which the Austrian emissaries departed, that Suleyman, brooding on his throne, raised his lean head and beckoned his Grand Vizier Ibrahim, who approached with confidence. The Grand Vizier was always sure of his master's approbation; was he not cup-companion and boyhood comrade of the Sultan?

Ibrahim had but one rival in his master's favor—the red-haired Russian girl, Khurrem the Joyous, whom Europe knew as Roxelana, whom slavers had dragged from her father's house in Rogatino to be the Sultan's *harim* favorite.

"I remember the infidel at last," said Suleyman. "Do you recall the first charge of the knights at Mohacz?"

Ibrahim winced slightly at the allusion.

"Oh, Protector of the Pitiful, is it likely that I should forget an occasion on which the divine blood of my master was spilt by an unbeliever?"

"Then you remember that thirty-two knights, the paladins of the Nazarenes, drove headlong into our array, each having pledged his life to cut down our person. By Allah, they rode like men riding to a wedding, their great horses and long lances overthrowing all who opposed them, and their plate-armor turned the finest steel. Yet they fell as the firelocks spoke until only three were left in the saddle—the knight Marczali and two companions. These paladins cut down my Solaks like ripe grain, but Marczali and one of his companions fell—almost at my feet.

"Yet one knight remained, though his vizored helmet had been torn from his head and blood started from every joint in his armor. He rode full at me, swinging his great two-handed sword, and I swear by the beard of the Prophet, death was so nigh me that I felt the burning breath of Azrael on my neck!

"His sword flashed like lightning in the sky, and glancing from my casque, whereby I was half-stunned so that blood gushed from my nose, rent the mail on my shoulder and gave me this wound, which irks me yet when the rains come. The Janizaries who swarmed around him cut the hocks of his horse, which brought him to earth as it went down, and the remnants of my Solaks bore me back out of the melee. Then the Hungarian host came on, and I saw not what became of the knight. But today I saw him again."

Ibrahim started with an exclamation of incredulity.

"Nay, I could not mistake those blue eyes. How it is I know not, but the knight that wounded me at Mohacz was this German, Gottfried von Kalmbach."

"But, Defender of the Faith," protested Ibrahim, "the heads of those

dog-knights were heaped before thy royal pavilion—"
"And I counted them and said nothing at the time, lest men think I held thee in blame," answered Suleyman. "There were but thirty-one. Most were so mutilated I could tell little of the features. But somehow the infidel escaped, who gave me this blow. I love brave men, but our blood is not so common that an unbeliever may with impunity spill it on the ground for the dogs to lap up. See ye to it."
Ibrahim salaamed deeply and withdrew. He made his way through broad corridors to a blue-tiled chamber whose gold-arched windows looked out on broad galleries, shaded by cypress and plane-trees, and cooled by the spray of silvery fountains. There at his summons came one Yaruk Khan, a Crim Tatar, a slant-eyed impassive figure in harness of lacquered leather and burnished bronze.
"Dog-brother," said the Vizier, "did thy koumiss-clouded gaze mark the tall German lord who served the emir Habordansky—the lord whose hair is tawny as a lion's mane?"
"Aye, *noyon,* he who is called Gombuk."
"The same. Take a *chambul* of thy dog-brothers and go after the Franks. Bring back this man and thou shalt be rewarded. The persons of envoys are sacred, but this matter is not official," he added cynically.
"To hear is to obey!" With a salaam as profound as that accorded to the Sultan himself, Yaruk Khan backed out of the presence of the second man of the empire.

He returned some days later, dusty, travel-stained, and without his prey. On him Ibrahim bent an eye full of menace, and the Tatar prostrated himself before the silken cushions on which the Grand Vizier sat, in the blue chamber with the gold-arched windows.
"Great khan, let not thine anger consume thy slave. The fault was not mine, by the beard of the Prophet."
"Squat on thy mangy haunches and bay out the tale," ordered Ibrahim considerately.
"Thus it was, my lord," began Yaruk Khan. "I rode swiftly, and though the Franks and their escort had a long start, and pushed on through the night without halting, I came up with them the next midday. But lo, Gombuk was not among them, and when I inquired after him, the paladin Habordansky replied only with many great oaths, like to the roaring of a cannon. So I spoke with various of the escort who understood the speech of these infidels, and learned what had come to pass. Yet I would have my lord remember that I only repeat the

words of the Spahis of the escort, who are men without honor and lie like—"

"Like a Tatar," said Ibrahim.

Yaruk Khan acknowledged the compliment with a wide dog-like grin, and continued.

"This they told me. At dawn Gombuk drew horse away from the rest, and the emir Habordansky demanded of him the reason. Then Gombuk laughed in the manner of the Franks—huh! huh! huh!—so.

"And Gombuk said: 'The devil of good your service has done me, so I cool my heels for nine months in a Turkish prison. Suleyman has given us safe conduct over the border and I am not compelled to ride with you.'

"'You dog,' said the emir, 'there is war in the wind and the Archduke has need of your sword.'

"'Devil eat the Archduke,' answered Gombuk; 'Zapolya is a dog because he stood aside at Mohacz, and let us, his comrades, be cut to pieces, but Ferdinand is a dog too. When I am penniless I sell him my sword. Now I have two hundred ducats and these robes which I can sell to any Jew for a handful of silver, and may the devil bite me if I draw sword for any man while I have a penny left. I'm for the nearest Christian tavern, and you and the Archduke may go to the devil.'

"Then the emir cursed him with many great curses, and Gombuk rode away laughing, huh! huh! huh!, and singing a song about a cockroach named—"

"Enough!" Ibrahim's features were dark with rage. He plucked savagely at his beard, reflecting that in the allusion to Mohacz, von Kalmbach had practically clinched Suleyman's suspicion. That matter of thirty-one heads when there should have been thirty-two was something no Turkish sultan would be likely to overlook. Officials had lost positions and their own heads over more trivial matters. The manner in which Suleyman had acted showed his almost incredible fondness and consideration for his Grand Vizier, but Ibrahim, vain though he was, was shrewd and wished no slightest shadow to come between him and his sovereign.

"Could you not have tracked him down, dog?" he demanded.

"By Allah," swore the uneasy Tatar, "he must have ridden on the wind. He crossed the border hours ahead of me, and I followed him as far as I dared—"

"Enough of excuses," interrupted Ibrahim. "Send Mikhal Oglu to me."

The Tatar departed thankfully. Ibrahim was not tolerant of failure in any man.

The Grand Vizier brooded on his silken cushions until the shadow of a pair The Grand Vizier brooded on his silken cushions until the shadow of a pair of vulture wings fell across the marble-tiled floor, and the lean figure he had summoned bowed before him. The man whose very name was a shuddering watchword of horror to all western Asia was soft-spoken and moved with the mincing ease of a cat, but the stark evil of his soul showed in his dark countenance, gleamed in his narrow slit eyes.
He was the chief of the Akinji, those wild riders whose raids spread fear and desolation throughout all lands beyond the Grand Turk's borders. He stood in full armor, a jeweled helmet on his narrow head, the wide vulture wings made fast to the shoulders of his gilded chain-mail hauberk. Those wings spread wide in the wind when he rode, and under their pinions lay the shadows of death and destruction. It was Suleyman's scimitar-tip, the most noted slayer of a nation of slayers, who stood before the Grand Vizier.
"Soon you will precede the hosts of our master into the lands of the infidel," said Ibrahim. "It will be your order, as always, to strike and spare not. You will waste the fields and the vineyards of the Caphars, you will burn their villages, you will strike down their men with arrows, and lead away their wenches captive. Lands beyond our line of march will cry out beneath your heel."
"That is good hearing, Favored of Allah," answered Mikhal Oglu in his soft courteous voice.
"Yet there is an order within the order," continued Ibrahim, fixing a piercing eye on the Akinji. "You know the German, von Kalmbach?"
"Aye—Gombuk as the Tatars call him."
"So. This is my command—whoever fights or flees, lives or dies—this man must not live. Search him out wherever he lies, though the hunt carry you to the very banks of the Rhine. When you bring me his head, your reward shall be thrice its weight in gold."
"To hear is to obey, my lord. Men say he is the vagabond son of a noble German family, whose ruin has been wine and women. They say he was once a Knight of Saint John, until cast forth for guzzling and—"
"Yet do not underrate him," answered Ibrahim grimly. "Sot he may be, but if he rode with Marczali, he is not to be despised. See thou to it!"
"There is no den where he can hide from me, oh Favored of Allah,"

declared Mikhal Oglu, "no night dark enough to conceal him, no forest thick enough. If I bring you not his head, I give him leave to send you mine."

"Enough!" Ibrahim grinned and tugged at his beard, well pleased. "You have my leave to go."

The sinister vulture-winged figure went springily and silently from the blue chamber, nor could Ibrahim guess that he was taking the first steps in a feud which should spread over years and far lands, swirling in dark tides to draw in thrones and kingdoms and red-haired women more beautiful than the flames of hell.

CHAPTER 2

IN A SMALL thatched hut in a village not far from the Danube, lusty snores resounded where a figure reclined in state on a ragged cloak thrown over a heap of straw. It was the paladin Gottfried von Kalmbach who slept the sleep of innocence and ale. The velvet vest, voluminous silken trousers, khalat and shagreen boots, gifts from a contemptuous sultan, were nowhere in evidence. The paladin was clad in worn leather and rusty mail. Hands tugged at him, breaking his sleep, and he swore drowsily.

"Wake up, my lord! Oh, wake, good knight—good pig—good dog-soul—will you wake, then?"

"Fill my flagon, host," mumbled the slumberer. "Who?—what? May the dogs bite you, Ivga! I've not another asper—not a penny. Go off like a good lass and let me sleep."

The girl renewed her tugging and shaking.

"Oh dolt! Rise! Gird on your spit! There are happenings forward!"

"Ivga," muttered Gottfried, pulling away from her attack, "take my burganet to the Jew. He'll give you enough for it to get drunk again."

"Fool!" she cried in despair. "It isn't money I want! The whole east is aflame, and none knows the reason thereof!"

"Has the rain ceased?" asked von Kalmbach, taking some interest in the proceedings at last.

"The rain ceased hours ago. You can only hear the drip from the thatch. Put on your sword and come out into the street. The men of the village are all drunk on your last silver, and the women know not what to think or do. Ah!"

The exclamation was broken from her by the sudden upleaping of a weird illumination which shone through the crevices of the hut. The German got unsteadily to his feet, quickly girt on the great two-handed sword and stuck his dented burganet on his cropped locks. Then he followed the girl into the straggling street. She was a slender young thing, barefooted, clad only in a short tunic-like garment, through the wide rents of which gleamed generous expanses of white flesh.

There seemed no life or movement in the village. Nowhere showed a light. Water dripped steadily from the eaves of the thatched roofs. Puddles in the muddy streets gleamed black. Wind sighed and moaned eerily through the black sodden branches of the trees which pressed in bulwarks of darkness about the little village, and in the southeast, towering higher into the leaden sky, rose the lurid crimson glow that set the dank clouds to smoldering. The girl Ivga cringed close to the tall German, whimpering.

"I'll tell you what it is, my girl," said he, scanning the glow. "It's Suleyman's devils. They've crossed the river and they're burning the villages. Aye, I've seen glares like that in the sky before. I've expected him before now, but these cursed rains we've had for weeks must have held him back. Aye, it's the Akinji, right enough, and they won't stop this side of Vienna. Look you, my girl, go quickly and quietly to the stable behind the hut and bring me my gray stallion. We'll slip out like mice from between the devil's fingers. The stallion will carry us both, easily."

"But the people of the village!" she sobbed, wringing her hands.

"Eh, well," he said, "God rest them; the men have drunk my ale valiantly and the women have been kind—but horns of Satan, girl, the gray nag won't carry a whole village!"

"Go you!" she returned. "I'll stay and die with my people!"

"The Turks won't kill you," he answered. "They'll sell you to a fat old Stamboul merchant who'll beat you. I won't stay to be cut open, and neither shall you—"

A terrible scream from the girl cut him short and he wheeled at the awful terror in her flaring eyes. Even as he did so, a hut at the lower end of the village sprang into flames, the sodden material burning slowly. A medley of screams and maddened yells followed the cry of the girl. In the sluggish light figures danced and capered wildly. Gottfried, straining his eyes in the shadows, saw shapes swarming over the low mud wall which drunkenness and negligence had left unguarded.

"Damnation!" he muttered. "The accursed ones have ridden ahead of their fire. They've stolen on the village in the dark—come on, girl!"

But even as he caught her white wrist to drag her away, and she screamed and fought against him like a wild thing, mad with fear, the mud wall crashed at the point nearest them. It crumpled under the impact of a score of horses, and into the doomed village reined the riders, distinct in the growing light. Huts were flaring up on all hands, screams rising to the dripping clouds as the invaders dragged shrieking women and drunken men from their hovels and cut their throats. Gottfried saw the lean figures of the horsemen, the firelight gleaming on their burnished steel; he saw the vulture wings on the shoulders of the foremost. Even as he recognized Mikhal Oglu, he saw the chief stiffen and point.

"At him, dogs!" yelled the Akinji, his voice no longer soft, but strident as the rasp of a drawn saber. "It is Gombuk! Five hundred aspers to the man who brings me his head!"

With a curse von Kalmbach bounded for the shadows of the nearest hut, dragging the screaming girl with him. Even as he leaped he heard the twang of bowstrings, and the girl sobbed and went limp in his grasp. She sank down at his feet, and in the lurid glare he saw the feathered end of an arrow quivering under her heart. With a low rumble he turned toward his assailants as a fierce bear turns at bay. An instant he stood, head out-thrust truculently, sword gripped in both hands; then, as a bear gives back from the onset of the hunters, he turned and fled about the hut, arrows whistling about him and glancing from the rings of his mail. There were no shots; the ride through that dripping forest had dampened the powder-flasks of the raiders.

Von Kalmbach quartered about the back of the hut, mindful of the fierce yells behind him, and gained the shed behind the hut he had occupied, wherein he stabled his gray stallion. Even as he reached the door, someone snarled like a panther in the semi-dark and cut viciously at him. He parried the stroke with the lifted sword and struck back with all the power of his broad shoulders. The great blade glanced stunningly from the Akinji's polished helmet and rent through the mail links of his hauberk, tearing arm from shoulder.

The Muhammadan sank down with a groan, and the German sprang over his prostrate form. The gray stallion, wild with fear and excitement, neighed shrilly and reared as his master sprang on his back. No time for saddle or bridle. Gottfried dug his heels into the quivering flanks and the great steed shot through the door like a thunderbolt, knocking men right and left like tenpins. Across the firelit open space between the burning huts he raced, clearing crumpled corpses in his stride, splashing his rider from heel to head as he thrashed through the puddles.

The Akinji made after the flying rider, loosing their shafts and giving tongue like hounds. Those mounted spurred after him, while those who had entered the village on foot ran through the broken wall for their horses.

Arrows flickered about Gottfried's head as he put his steed at the only point open to him—the unbroken western wall. It was touch and go, for the footing was tricky and treacherous and never had the gray stallion attempted such a leap. Gottfried held his breath as he felt the great body beneath him gathering and tensing in full flight for the desperate effort; then with a volcanic heave of mighty thews the stallion rose in the air and cleared the barrier with scarce an inch to spare.

The pursuers yelled in amazement and fury, and reined back. Born horsemen though they were, they dared not attempt that breakneck leap. They lost time seeking gates and breaks in the wall, and when they finally emerged from the village, the black, dank, whispering, dripping forest had swallowed up their prey.

Mikhal Oglu swore like a fiend and leaving his lieutenant Othman in charge with instructions to leave no living human being in the village, he pressed on after the fugitive, following the trail, by torches, in the muddy mold, and swearing to run him down, if the road led under the very walls of Vienna.

CHAPTER 3

ALLAH did not will it that Mikhal Oglu should take Gottfried von Kalmbach's head in the dark, dripping forest. He knew the country better than they, and in spite of their zeal, they lost his trail in the darkness.

Dawn found Gottfried riding through terror-stricken farmlands, with the flame of a burning world lighting the east and south. The country was thronged with fugitives, staggering under pitiful loads of household goods, driving bellowing cattle, like people fleeing the end of the world. The torrential rains that had offered false promise of security had not long stayed the march of the Grand Turk.

With a quarter-million followers he was ravaging the eastern marches of Christendom. While Gottfried had loitered in the taverns of isolated villages, drinking up the Sultan's bounty, Pesth and Buda had fallen, the German soldiers of the latter having been slaughtered by the Janizaries, after promises of safety sworn by Suleyman, whom men named the Generous.

While Ferdinand and the nobles and bishops squabbled at the Diet of Spires, the elements alone seemed to war for Christendom. Rain fell in torrents, and through the floods that changed plains and forest-bed to dank morasses, the Turks struggled grimly. They drowned in raging rivers, and lost great stores of ammunition, ordnance and supplies when boats capsized, bridges gave way, and wagons mired. But on they came, driven by the implacable will of Suleyman, and now in September, 1529, over the ruins of Hungary, the Turk swept on Europe, with the Akinji—the Sackmen—ravaging the land like the drift ahead of a storm.

This in part Gottfried learned from the fugitives as he pushed his weary stallion toward the city which was the only sanctuary for the panting thousands. Behind him the skies flamed red and the screams of butchered victims came dimly down the wind to his ears. Sometimes he could even make out the swarming black masses of wild horsemen. The wings of the vulture beat horrifically over that butchered land and the shadows of those great wings fell across all Europe. Again the destroyer was riding out of the blue mysterious East as his brothers had ridden before him—Attila—Subotai—Bayazid—Muhammad the Conqueror. But never before had such a storm risen against the West.

Before the waving vulture wings the road thronged with wailing fugitives; behind them it ran red and silent, strewn with mangled shapes that cried no more. The killers were not a half-hour behind him when Gottfried von Kalmbach rode his reeling stallion through the gates of Vienna. The people on the walls had heard the wailing for hours, rising awfully on the wind, and now afar they saw the sun flicker on the points of lances as the horsemen rode in amongst the masses of fugitives toiling down from the hills into the plain which girdles the city. They saw the play of naked steel like sickles among ripe grain.

Von Kalmbach found the city in turmoil, the people swirling and screaming about Count Nikolas Salm, the seventy-year-old warhorse who commanded Vienna, and his aides, Roggendrof, Count Nikolas Zrinyi and Paul Bakics. Salm was working with frantic haste, leveling houses near the walls and using their material to brace the ramparts, which were old and unstable, nowhere more than six feet thick, and in many places crumbling and falling down. The outer palisade was so frail it bore the name of Stadtzaun—city hedge.

But under the lashing energy of Count Salm, a new wall twenty feet high was thrown up from the Stuben to the Karnthner Gate. Ditches interior to the old moat were dug, and ramparts erected from the drawbridge to the Salz Gate. Roofs were stripped of shingles, to lessen the chances of fire, and paving was ripped up to soften the impact of cannonballs.

The suburbs had been deserted, and now they were fired lest they give shelter to the besiegers. In the process, which was carried out in the very teeth of the oncoming Sackmen, conflagrations broke out in the city and added to the delirium.

It was all hell and bedlam turned loose, and in the midst of it, five thousand wretched noncombatants, old men and women, and children, were ruthlessly driven from the gates to shift for themselves, and their screams, as the Akinjis swooped down, maddened the people within the walls.

These hellions were arriving by thousands, topping the skylines, and sweeping down on the city in irregular squadrons, like vultures gathering about a dying camel.

Within an hour after the first swarm had appeared, not one Christian remained alive outside the gates, except those bound by long ropes to the saddle-peaks of their captors and forced to run at full speed or be dragged to death.

The wild riders swirled about the walls, yelling and loosing their shafts. Men on the towers recognized the dread Mikhal Oglu by the wings on his cuirass, and noted that he rode from one heap of dead to another, avidly scanning each corpse in turn, pausing to glare questioningly at the battlements.

Meanwhile, from the west, a band of German and Spanish troops cut their way through a cordon of Sackmen and marched into the streets to the accompaniment of frenzied cheers, Philip the Palgrave at their head.

Gottfried von Kalmbach leaned on his sword and watched them pass in their gleaming breastplates and plumed crested helmets, with long matchlocks on their shoulders and two-handed swords strapped to their steel-clad backs. He was a curious contrast in his rusty chain-mail, old-fashioned harness picked up here and there and slovenly pieced together—he seemed like a figure out of the past, rusty and tarnished, watching a newer, brighter generation go by. Yet Philip saluted him, with a glance of recognition, as the shining column swung past.

Von Kalmbach started toward the walls, where the gunners were firing frugally at the Akinji, who showed some disposition to climb upon the bastions on lariats thrown from their saddles. But on the way he heard that Salm was impressing nobles and soldiers in the task of digging moats and rearing new earthworks, and in great haste he took refuge in a tavern, where he bullied the host, a knock-kneed and apprehensive Wallachian, into giving him credit, and rapidly drank himself into a state where no one would have considered asking him to do work of any kind.

Shots, shouts and screams reached his ears, but he paid scant heed. He knew that the Akinji would strike and pass on, to ravage the country beyond. He learned from the tavern talk that Salm had 20,000 pikemen, 2,000 horsemen and 1,000 volunteer citizens to oppose Suleyman's hordes, together with seventy guns—cannons, demi-cannons and culverins.

The news of the Turks' numbers numbed all hearts with dread—all but von Kalmbach's. He was a fatalist in his way. But he discovered a conscience in ale, and was presently brooding over the people the miserable Viennese had driven forth to perish. The more he drank the more melancholy he became, and maudlin tears dripped from the drooping ends of his mustaches.

At last he rose unsteadily and took up his great sword, muzzily intent on challenging Count Salm to a duel because of the matter. He bellowed down the timid importunities of the Wallachian and weaved out on the street. To his groggy sight the towers and spires cavorted crazily; people jostled him, knocking him aside as they ran about aimlessly. Philip the Palgrave strode by clanking in his armor, the keen dark faces of his Spaniards contrasting with the square, florid countenances of the Lanzknechts.

"Shame upon you, von Kalmbach!" said Philip sternly. "The Turk is upon us, and you keep your snout shoved in an ale-pot!"

"Whose snout is in what ale-pot?" demanded Gottfried, weaving in an erratic half-circle as he fumbled at his sword. "Devil bite you, Philip, I'll rap your pate for that—"

The Palgrave was already out of sight, and eventually Gottfried found himself on the Karnthner Tower, only vaguely aware of how he had got there. But what he saw sobered him suddenly. The Turk was indeed upon Vienna. The plain was covered with his tents, thirty thousand, some said, and swore that from the lofty spire of Saint Stephen's cathedral a man could not see their limits. Four hundred of his boats lay on the Danube, and Gottfried heard men cursing the Austrian fleet which lay helpless far upstream, because its sailors, long unpaid, refused to man the ships. He also heard that Salm had made no reply at all to Suleyman's demand to surrender.

Now, partly as a gesture, partly to awe the Caphar dogs, the Grand Turk's array was moving in orderly procession before the ancient walls before settling down to the business of the siege. The sight was enough to awe the stoutest. The low-swinging sun struck fire from polished helmet, jeweled saber-hilt and lance-point. It was as if a river of shining steel flowed leisurely and terribly past the walls of Vienna. The Akinji, who ordinarily formed the vanguard of the host, had swept on, but in their place rode the Tatars of Crimea, crouching on their high-peaked, short-stirruped saddles, their gnome-like heads guarded by iron helmets, their stocky bodies with bronze breastplates and lacquered leather. Behind them came the Azabs, the irregular infantry, Kurds and Arabs for the most part, a wild, motley horde. Then their brothers, the Delis, the Madcaps, wild men on tough ponies fantastically adorned with fur and feathers. The riders wore caps and mantles of leopard skin; their unshorn hair hung in tangled strands about their high shoulders, and over their matted beards their eyes glared the madness of fanaticism and bhang.

After them came the real body of the army. First the beys and emirs with their retainers—horsemen and footmen from the feudal fiefs of Asia Minor. Then the Spahis, the heavy cavalry, on splendid steeds. And last of all the real strength of the Turkish empire—the most terrible military organization in the world—the Janizaries.

On the walls men spat in black fury, recognizing kindred blood. For the Janizaries were not Turks. With a few exceptions, where Turkish parents had smuggled their offspring into the ranks to save them from the grinding life of a peasant, they were sons of Christians—Greeks, Serbs, Hungarians—stolen in infancy and raised in the ranks of Islam, knowing but one master—the Sultan; but one occupation—slaughter. Their beardless features contrasted with those of their Oriental masters. Many had blue eyes and yellow mustaches. But all their faces were stamped with the wolfish ferocity to which they had been reared. Under their dark blue cloaks glinted fine mail, and many wore steel skull-caps under their curious, high-peaked hats from which depended a white sleeve-like piece of cloth, and through which was thrust a copper spoon. Long bird-of-paradise plumes likewise adorned these strange head-pieces.

Besides scimitars, pistols and daggers, each Janizary bore a matchlock, and their officers carried pots of coals for the lighting of the matches. Up and down the ranks scurried the dervishes, clad only in kalpaks of camel-hair and green aprons fringed with ebony beads, exhorting the Faithful. Military bands, the invention of the Turk, marched with the columns, cymbals clashing, lutes twanging. Over the flowing sea the banners tossed and swayed—the crimson flag of the Spahis, the white banner of the Janizaries with its two-edged sword worked in gold, and the horse-tail standards of the rulers—seven tails for the Sultan, six for the Grand Vizier, three for the Agha of the Janizaries. So Suleyman paraded his power before despairing Caphar eyes.

But von Kalmbach's gaze was centered on the groups that labored to set up the ordnance of the Sultan. And he shook his head in bewilderment.

"Demi-culverins, sakers, and falconets!" he grunted. "Where the devil's all the heavy artillery Suleyman's so proud of?"

"At the bottom of the Danube!" A Hungarian pikeman grinned fiercely and spat as he answered. "Wulf Hagen sank that part of the Soldan's flotilla. The rest of his cannon and cannon royal, they say, were mired because of the rains."

A slow grin bristled Gottfried's mustache.

"What was Suleyman's word to Salm?"

"That he'd eat breakfast in Vienna day after tomorrow—the 29th."

Gottfried shook his head ponderously.

CHAPTER 4

THE SIEGE COMMENCED, with the roaring of cannons, the whistling of arrows, and the blasting crash of matchlocks. The Janizaries took possession of the ruined suburbs, where fragments of walls gave them shelter. Under a screen of irregulars and a volley of arrow-fire, they advanced methodically just after dawn.

On a gun-turret on the threatened wall, leaning on his great sword and meditatively twisting his mustache, Gottfried von Kalmbach watched a Transylvanian gunner being carried off the wall, his brains oozing from a hole in his head; a Turkish matchlock had spoken too near the walls.

The field-pieces of the Sultan were barking like deep-toned dogs, knocking chips off the battlements. The Janizaries were advancing, kneeling, firing, reloading as they came on. Bullets glanced from the crenelles and whined off venomously into space. One flattened against Gottfried's hauberk, bringing an outraged grunt from him. Turning toward the abandoned gun, he saw a colorful, incongruous figure bending over the massive breech.

It was a woman, dressed as von Kalmbach had not seen even the dandies of France dressed. She was tall, splendidly shaped, but lithe. From under a steel cap escaped rebellious tresses that rippled red gold in the sun over her compact shoulders. High boots of Cordovan leather came to her mid-thighs, which were cased in baggy breeches. She wore a shirt of fine Turkish mesh-mail tucked into her breeches. Her supple waist was confined by a flowing sash of green silk, into which were thrust a brace of pistols and a dagger, and from which depended a long Hungarian saber. Over all was carelessly thrown a scarlet cloak.

This surprizing figure was bending over the cannon, sighting it in a manner betokening more than a passing familiarity, at a group of Turks who were wheeling a carriage-gun just within range.

"Eh, Red Sonya!" shouted a man-at-arms, waving his pike. "Give 'em hell, my lass!"

"Trust me, dog-brother," she retorted as she applied the glowing match to the vent. "But I wish my mark was Roxelana's—"

A terrific detonation drowned her words and a swirl of smoke blinded every one on the turret, as the terrific recoil of the overcharged cannon knocked the firer flat on her back. She sprang up like a spring rebounding and rushed to the embrasure, peering eagerly through the smoke, which clearing, showed the ruin of the gun crew. The huge ball, bigger than a man's head, had smashed full into the group clustered about the saker, and now they lay on the torn ground, their skulls blasted by the impact, or their bodies mangled by the flying iron splinters from their shattered gun. A cheer went up from the towers, and the woman called Red Sonya yelled with a sincere joy and did the steps of a Cossack dance.

Gottfried approached, eying in open admiration the splendid swell of her bosom beneath the pliant mail, the curves of her ample hips and rounded limbs. She stood as a man might stand, booted legs braced wide apart, thumbs hooked into her girdle, but she was all woman. She was laughing as she faced him, and he noted with fascination the dancing sparkling lights and changing colors of her eyes. She raked back her rebellious locks with a powder-stained hand and he

wondered at the clear pinky whiteness of her firm flesh where it was unstained.
"Why did you wish for the Sultana Roxelana for a target, my girl?" he asked.
"Because she's my sister, the slut!" answered Sonya.
At that instant a great cry thundered over the walls and the girl started like a wild thing, ripping out her blade in a long flash of silver in the sun.
"That bellow!" she cried. "The Janizaries—"
Gottfried was already on his way to the embrasures. He too had heard before the terrible soul-shaking shout of the charging Janizaries. Suleyman meant to waste no time on the city that barred him from helpless Europe. He meant to crush its frail walls in one storm. The bashi-bazouki, the irregulars, died like flies to screen the main advance, and over heaps of their dead, the Janizaries thundered against Vienna. In the teeth of cannonade and musket volley they surged on, crossing the moats on scaling-ladders laid across, bridge-like. Whole ranks went down as the Austrian guns roared, but now the attackers were under the walls and the cumbrous balls whirred over their heads, to work havoc in the rear ranks.
The Spanish matchlock men, firing almost straight down, took ghastly toll, but now the ladders gripped the walls, and the chanting madmen surged upward. Arrows whistled, striking down the defenders. Behind them the Turkish field-pieces boomed, careless of injury to friend as well as foe. Gottfried, standing at an embrasure, was overthrown by a sudden terrific impact. A ball had smashed the merlon, braining half a dozen defenders.
Gottfried rose, half-stunned, out of the debris of masonry and huddled corpses. He looked down into an uprushing waste of snarling, impassioned faces, where eyes glared like mad dogs' and blades glittered like sunbeams on water. Bracing his feet wide, he heaved up his great sword and lashed down. His jaw jutted out, his mustache bristled. The five-foot blade caved in steel caps and skulls, lashing through uplifted bucklers and iron shoulder-pieces. Men fell from the ladders, their nerveless fingers slipping from the bloody rungs.
But they swarmed through the breach on either side of him. A terrible cry announced that the Turks had a foothold on the wall. But no man dared leave his post to go to the threatened point. To the dazed defenders it seemed that Vienna was ringed by a glittering, tossing sea

that roared higher and higher about the doomed walls.

Stepping back to avoid being hemmed in, Gottfried grunted and lashed right and left. His eyes were no longer cloudy; they blazed like blue balefire. Three Janizaries were down at his feet; his broadsword clanged in a forest of slashing scimitars. A blade splintered on his basinet, filling his eyes with fire-shot blackness. Staggering, he struck back and felt his great blade crunch home. Blood jetted over his hands and he tore his sword clear. Then with a yell and a rush someone was at his side and he heard the quick splintering of mail beneath the madly flailing strokes of a saber that flashed like silver lightning before his clearing sight.

It was Red Sonya who had come to his aid, and her onslaught was no less terrible than that of a she-panther. Her strokes followed each other too quickly for the eye to follow; her blade was a blur of white fire, and men went down like ripe grain before the reaper. With a deep roar Gottfried strode to her side, bloody and terrible, swinging his great blade. Forced irresistibly back, the Moslems wavered on the edge of the wall, then leaped for the ladders or fell screaming through empty space.

Oaths flowed in a steady stream from Sonya's red lips and she laughed wildly as her saber sang home and blood spurted along the edge. The last Turk on the battlement screamed and parried wildly as she pressed him; then dropping his scimitar, his clutching hands closed desperately on her dripping blade. With a groan he swayed on the edge, blood gushing from his horribly cut fingers.

"Hell to you, dog-soul!" she laughed. "The devil can stir your broth for you!"

With a twist and a wrench she tore away her saber, severing the wretch's fingers; with a moaning cry he pitched backward and fell headlong.

On all sides the Janizaries were falling back. The field-pieces, halted while the fighting went on upon the walls, were booming again, and the Spaniards, kneeling at the embrasures, were returning the fire with their long matchlocks.

Gottfried approached Red Sonya, who was cleansing her blade, swearing softly.

"By God, my girl," said he, extending a huge hand, "had you not come to my aid, I think I'd have supped in Hell this night. I thank—"

"Thank the devil!" retorted Sonya rudely, slapping his hand aside. "The Turks were on the wall. Don't think I risked my hide to save

yours, dog-brother!"
And with a scornful flirt of her wide coattails, she swaggered off down the battlements, giving back promptly and profanely the rude sallies of the soldiers. Gottfried scowled after her, and a Lanzknecht slapped him jovially on the shoulder.
"Eh, she's a devil, that one! She drinks the strongest head under the table and outswears a Spaniard. She's no man's light o' love. Cut—slash —death to you, dog-soul! There's her way."
"Who is she, in the devil's name?" growled von Kalmbach.
"Red Sonya from Rogatino—that's all we know. Marches and fights like a man—God knows why. Swears she's sister to Roxelana, the Soldan's favorite. If the Tatars who grabbed Roxelana that night had got Sonya, by Saint Piotr! Suleyman would have had a handful! Let her alone, sir brother; she's a wildcat. Come and have a tankard of ale."

The Janizaries, summoned before the Grand Vizier to explain why the attack failed after the wall had been scaled at one place, swore they had been confronted by a devil in the form of a red-headed woman, aided by a giant in rusty mail.
Ibrahim discounted the woman, but the description of the man woke a half-forgotten memory in his mind. After dismissing the soldiers, he summoned the Tatar, Yaruk Khan, and dispatched him up-country to demand of Mikhal Oglu why he had not sent a certain head to the royal tent.

CHAPTER 5

SULEYMAN did not eat his breakfast in Vienna on the morning of the 29th. He stood on the height of Semmering, before his rich pavilion with its gold-knobbed pinnacles and its guard of five hundred Solaks, and watched his light batteries pecking away vainly at the frail walls; he saw his irregulars wasting their lives like water, striving to fill the fosse, and he saw his sappers burrowing like moles, driving mines and counter-mines nearer and nearer the bastions.
Within the city there was little ease. Night and day the walls were manned. In their cellars the Viennese watched the faint vibrations of peas on drumheads that betrayed the sounds of digging in the earth. They told of Turkish mines burrowing under the walls, and sank their counter-mines, accordingly. Men fought no less fiercely under the earth than above.
Vienna was the one Christian island in a sea of infidels. Night by night

men watched the horizons burning where the Akinji yet scoured the agonized land. Occasionally word came from the outer world—slaves escaping from the camp to slipping into the city. Always their news was fresh horror. In Upper Austria less than a third of the inhabitants were left alive; Mikhal Oglu was outdoing himself. And the people said that it was evident the vulture-winged one was looking for one in particular. His slayers brought men's heads and heaped them high before him; he avidly searched among the grisly relics, then, apparently in fiendish disappointment, drove his devils to new atrocities.

These tales, instead of paralyzing the Austrians with dread, fired them with the mad fury of desperation. Mines exploded, breaches were made and the Turks swarmed in, but always the desperate Christians were there before them, and in the choking, blind, wild-beast madness of hand-to-hand fighting they paid in part the red debt they owed.

September dwindled into October; the leaves turned brown and yellow on Wiener Wald, and the winds blew cold. The watchers shivered at night on the walls that whitened to the bite of the frost; but still the tents ringed the city; and still Suleyman sat in his magnificent pavilion and glared at the frail barrier that barred his imperial path. None but Ibrahim dared speak to him; his mood was black as the cold nights that crept down from the northern hills. The wind that moaned outside his tent seemed a dirge for his ambitions of conquest. Ibrahim watched him narrowly, and after a vain onset that lasted from dawn till midday, he called off the Janizaries and bade them retire into the ruined suburbs and rest. And he sent a bowman to shoot a very certain shaft into a very certain part of the city, where certain persons were waiting for just such an event.

No more attacks were made that day. The field-pieces, which had been pounding at the Karnthner Gate for days, were shifted northward, to hammer at the Burg. As an assault on that part of the wall seemed imminent, the bulk of the soldiery was shifted there. But the onslaught did not come, though the batteries kept up a steady fire, hour after hour. Whatever the reason, the soldiers gave thanks for the respite; they were dizzy with fatigue, mad with raw wounds and lack of sleep.

That night the great square, the Am-Hof market, seethed with soldiers, while civilians looked on enviously. A great store of wine had been discovered hidden in the cellars of a rich Jewish merchant, who hoped to reap triple profit when all other liquor in the city was gone. In spite of their officers, the half-crazed men rolled the great hogsheads into the square and broached them. Salm gave up the attempt to control them. Better drunkenness, growled the old warhorse, than for the men to fall in their tracks from exhaustion. He paid the Jew from his own purse. In relays the soldiers came from the walls and drank deep.

In the glare of cressets and torches, to the accompaniment of drunken shouts and songs, to which the occasional rumble of a cannon played a sinister undertone, von Kalmbach dipped his basinet into a barrel and brought it out brimful and dripping. Sinking his mustache into the liquid, he paused as his clouded eyes, over the rim of the steel cap, rested on a strutting figure on the other side of the hogshead. Resentment touched his expression. Red Sonya had already visited more than one barrel. Her burganet was thrust sidewise on her rebellious locks, her swagger was wilder, her eyes more mocking.

"Ha!" she cried scornfully. "It's the Turk-killer, with his nose deep in the keg, as usual! Devil bite all topers!"

She consistently thrust a jeweled goblet into the crimson flood and emptied it at a gulp. Gottfried stiffened resentfully. He had had a tilt with Sonya already, and he still smarted.

"Why should I even look at you, in your ragged harness and empty purse," she had mocked, "when even Paul Bakics is mad for me? Go along, guzzler, beer-keg!"

"Be damned to you," he had retorted. "You needn't be so high, just because your sister is the Soldan's mistress—"

At that she had flown into an awful passion, and they had parted with mutual curses. Now, from the devil in her eyes, he saw that she intended making things further uncomfortable for him.

"Hussy!" he growled. "I'll drown you in this hogshead."

"Nay, you'll drown yourself first, boar-pig!" she shouted amid a roar of rough laughter. "A pity you aren't as valiant against the Turks as you are against the wine-butts!"

"Dogs bite you, slut!" he roared. "How can I break their heads when they stand off and pound us with cannon balls? Shall I throw my dagger at them from the wall?"

"There are thousands just outside," she retorted in the madness induced by drink and her own wild nature, "if any had the guts to go to them."

"By God!" the maddened giant dragged out his great sword. "No baggage can call *me* coward, sot or not! I'll go out upon them, if never a man follow me!"

Bedlam followed his bellow; the drunken temper of the crowd was fit for such madness. The nearly empty hogsheads were deserted as men tipsily drew sword and reeled toward the outer gates.

Wulf Hagen fought his way into the storm, buffeting men right and left, shouting fiercely, "Wait, you drunken fools! Don't surge out in this shape! Wait—" They brushed him aside, sweeping on in a blind senseless torrent.

Dawn was just beginning to tip the eastern hills. Somewhere in the strangely silent Turkish camp a drum began to throb. Turkish sentries stared wildly and loosed their matchlocks in the air to warn the camp, appalled at the sight of the Christian horde pouring over the narrow drawbridge, eight thousand strong, brandishing swords and ale tankards. As they foamed over the moat a terrific explosion rent the din, and a portion of the wall near the Karnthner Gate seemed to detach itself and rise into the air. A great shout rose from the Turkish camp, but the attackers did not pause.

They rushed headlong into the suburbs, and there they saw the Janizaries, not rousing from slumber, but fully clad and armed, being hurriedly drawn up in charging lines. Without pausing, they burst headlong into the half-formed ranks. Far outnumbered, their drunken fury and velocity was yet irresistible. Before the madly thrashing axes and lashing broadswords, the Janizaries reeled back dazed and disordered. The suburbs became a shambles where battling men, slashing and hewing at one another, stumbled on mangled bodies and severed limbs. Suleyman and Ibrahim, on the height of Semmering, saw the invincible Janizaries in full retreat, streaming out toward the hills.

In the city the rest of the defenders were working madly to repair the great breach the mysterious explosion had torn in the wall. Salm gave thanks for that drunken sortie. But for it, the Janizaries would have been pouring through the breach before the dust settled.

All was confusion in the Turkish camp. Suleyman ran to his horse and took charge in person, shouting at the Spahis. They formed ranks and swung down the slopes in orderly squadrons. The Christian warriors, still following their fleeing enemies, suddenly awakened to their danger. Before them the Janizaries were still falling back, but on either flank the horsemen of Asia were galloping to cut them off.

Fear replaced drunken recklessness. They began to fall back, and the retreat quickly became a rout. Screaming in blind panic they threw away their weapons and fled for the drawbridge. The Turks rode them down to the water's edge, and tried to follow them across the bridge, into the gates which were opened for them. And there at the bridge Wulf Hagen and his retainers met the pursuers and held them hard. The flood of the fugitives flowed past him to safety; on him the Turkish tide broke like a red wave. He loomed, a steel-clad giant, in a waste of spears.

Gottfried von Kalmbach did not voluntarily quit the field, but the rush of his companions swept him along the tide of flight, blaspheming bitterly. Presently he lost his footing and his panic-stricken comrades stampeded across his prostrate frame. When the frantic heels ceased to drum on his mail, he raised his head and saw that he was near the fosse, and naught but Turks about him. Rising, he ran lumberingly toward the moat, into which he plunged unexpectedly, looking back over his shoulder at a pursuing Moslem.

He came up floundering and spluttering, and made for the opposite bank, splashing water like a buffalo. The blood-mad Muhammadan was close behind him—an Algerian corsair, as much at home in water as out. The stubborn German would not drop his great sword, and burdened by his mail, just managed to reach the other bank, where he clung, utterly exhausted and unable to lift a hand in defense as the Algerian swirled in, dagger gleaming above his naked shoulder. Then someone swore heartily on the bank hard by. A slim hand thrust a long pistol into the Algerian's face; he screamed as it exploded, making a ghastly ruin of his head. Another slim, strong hand gripped the sinking German by the scruff of his mail.

"Grab the bank, fool!" gritted a voice, indicative of great effort. "I can't heave you up alone; you must weigh a ton. Pull, dolt, pull!"

Blowing, gasping and floundering, Gottfried half-clambered, was half lifted, out of the moat. He showed some disposition to lie on his belly and retch, what of the dirty water he had swallowed, but his rescuer urged him to his feet.

"The Turks are crossing the bridge and the lads are closing the gates against them—haste, before we're cut off."

Inside the gate Gottfried stared about, as if waking from a dream.

"Where's Wulf Hagen? I saw him holding the bridge."

"Lying dead among twenty dead Turks," answered Red Sonya.

Gottfried sat down on a piece of fallen wall, and because he was shaken and exhausted, and still mazed with drink and blood-lust, he sank his face in his huge hands and wept. Sonya kicked him disgustedly.

"Name o' Satan, man, don't sit and blubber like a spanked schoolgirl. You drunkards had to play the fool, but that can't be mended. Come—let's go to the Walloon's tavern and drink ale."

"Why did you pull me out of the moat?" he asked.

"Because a great oaf like you never can help himself. I see you need a wise person like me to keep life in that hulking frame."

"But I thought you despised me!"

"Well, a woman can change her mind, can't she?" she snapped.

Along the walls the pikemen were repelling the frothing Moslems, thrusting them off the partly repaired breach. In the royal pavilion Ibrahim was explaining to his master that the devil had undoubtedly inspired that drunken sortie just at the right moment to spoil the Grand Vizier's carefully laid plans. Suleyman, wild with fury, spoke shortly to his friend for the first time.

"Nay, thou hast failed. Have done with thine intrigues. Where craft has failed, sheer force shall prevail. Send a rider for the Akinji; they are needed here to replace the fallen. Bid the hosts to the attack again."

CHAPTER 6

THE PRECEDING ONSLAUGHTS were naught to the storm that now burst on Vienna's reeling walls. Night and day the cannons flashed and thundered. Bombs burst on roofs and in the streets. When men died on the walls there was none to take their places. Fear of famine stalked the streets and the darker fear of treachery ran black-mantled through the alleys.

Investigation showed that the blast that had rent the Karnthner wall had not been fired from without. In a mine tunneled from an unsuspected cellar inside the city, a heavy charge of powder had been exploded beneath the wall. One or two men, working secretly, might have done it. It was now apparent that the bombardment of the Burg had been merely a gesture to draw attention away from the Karnthner wall, to give the traitors an opportunity to work undiscovered.

Count Salm and his aides did the work of giants. The aged commander, fired with superhuman energy, trod the walls, braced the faltering, aided the wounded, fought in the breaches side by side with the common soldiers, while death dealt his blows unsparingly.

But if death supped within the walls, he feasted full without. Suleyman drove his men as relentlessly as if he were their worst foe. Plague stalked among them, and the ravaged countryside yielded no food. The cold winds howled down from the Carpathians and the warriors shivered in their light Oriental garb. In the frosty nights the hands of the sentries froze to their matchlocks. The ground grew hard as flint and the sappers toiled feebly with blunted tools. Rain fell, mingled with sleet, extinguishing matches, wetting powder, turning the plain outside the city to a muddy wallow, where rotting corpses sickened the living.

Suleyman shuddered as with an ague, as he looked out over the camp. He saw his warriors, worn and haggard, toiling in the muddy plain like ghosts under the gloomy leaden skies. The stench of his slaughtered thousands was in his nostrils. In that instant it seemed to the Sultan that he looked on a gray plain of the dead, where corpses dragged their lifeless bodies to an outworn task, animated only by the ruthless will of their master. For an instant the Tatar in his veins rose above the Turk and he shook with fear. Then his lean jaws set. The walls of Vienna staggered drunkenly, patched and repaired in a score of places. How could they stand?

"Sound for the onslaught. Thirty thousand aspers to the first man on the walls!"

The Grand Vizier spread his hands helplessly. "The spirit is gone out of the warriors. They can not endure the miseries of this icy land."

"Drive them to the walls with whips," answered Suleyman, grimly. "This is the gate to Frankistan. It is through it we must ride the road to empire."

Drums thundered through the camp. The weary defenders of Christendom rose up and gripped their weapons, electrified by the instinctive knowledge that the death-grip had come.

In the teeth of roaring matchlocks and swinging broadswords, the officers of the Sultan drove the Moslem hosts. Whips cracked and men cried out blasphemously up and down the lines. Maddened, they hurled themselves at the reeling walls, riddled with great breaches, yet still barriers behind which desperate men could crouch. Charge after charge rolled on over the choked fosse, broke on the staggering walls, and rolled back, leaving its wash of dead. Night fell unheeded, and through the darkness, lighted by blaze of cannon and flare of torches, the battle raged. Driven by Suleyman's terrible will, the attackers fought throughout the night, heedless of all Moslem tradition.

Dawn rose as on Armageddon. Before the walls of Vienna lay a vast carpet of steel-clad dead. Their plumes waved in the wind. And across the corpses staggered the hollow-eyed attackers to grapple with the dazed defenders.

The steel tides rolled and broke, and rolled on again, till the very gods must have stood aghast at the giant capacity of men for suffering and enduring. It was the Armageddon of races—Asia against Europe. About the walls raved a sea of Eastern faces—Turks, Tatars, Kurds, Arabs, Algerians, snarling, screaming, dying before the roaring matchlocks of the Spaniards, the thrust of Austrian pikes, the strokes of the German Lanzknechts, who swung their two-handed swords like reapers mowing ripe grain. Those within the walls were no more heroic than those without, stumbling among fields of their own dead.

To Gottfried von Kalmbach, life had faded to a single meaning—the swinging of his great sword. In the wide breach by the Karnthner Tower he fought until time lost all meaning. For long ages maddened faces rose snarling before him, the faces of devils, and scimitars flashed before his eyes everlastingly. He did not feel his wounds, nor the drain of weariness. Gasping in the choking dust, blind with sweat and blood, he dealt death like a harvest, dimly aware that at his side a slim, pantherish figure swayed and smote— at first with laughter, curses and snatches of song, later in grim silence.

His identity as an individual was lost in that cataclysm of swords. He hardly knew it when Count Salm was death-stricken at his side by a bursting bomb. He was not aware when night crept over the hills, nor did he realize at last that the tide was slackening and ebbing. He was only dimly aware that Nikolas Zrinyi tore him away from the corpse-choked breach, saying, "God's name, man, go and sleep. We've beaten them off—for the time being, at least."

He found himself in a narrow, winding street, all dark and forsaken. He had no idea of how he had got there, but seemed vaguely to remember a hand on his elbow, tugging, guiding. The weight of his mail pulled at his sagging shoulders. He could not tell if the sound he heard were the cannon fitfully roaring, or a throbbing in his own head. It seemed there was someone he should look for—someone who meant a great deal to him. But all was vague. Somewhere, sometime, it seemed long, long ago, a sword-stroke had cleft his basinet. When he tried to think he seemed to feel again the impact of that terrible blow, and his brain swam. He tore off the dented head-piece and cast it into the street.

Again the hand was tugging at his arm. A voice urged, "Wine, my lord —drink!"

Dimly he saw a lean, black-mailed figure extending a tankard. With a gasp he caught at it and thrust his muzzle into the stinging liquor, gulping like a man dying of thirst. Then something burst in his brain. The night filled with a million flashing sparks, as if a powder magazine had exploded in his head. After that, darkness and oblivion.

He came slowly to himself, aware of a raging thirst, an aching head, and an intense weariness that seemed to paralyze his limbs. He was bound hand and foot, and gagged. Twisting his head, he saw that he was in a small bare dusty room, from which a winding stone stair led up. He deduced that he was in the lower part of the tower.

Over a guttering candle on a crude table stooped two men. They were both lean and hook-nosed, clad in plain black garments—Asiatics, past doubt.

Gottfried listened to their low-toned conversation. He had picked up many languages in his wanderings. He recognized them—Tshoruk and his son Rhupen, Armenian merchants. He remembered that he had seen Tshoruk often in the last week or so, ever since the domed helmets of the Akinji had appeared in Suleyman's camp. Evidently the merchant had been shadowing him, for some reason. Tshoruk was reading what he had written on a bit of parchment.

"My lord, though I blew up the Karnthner wall in vain, yet I have news to make my lord's heart glad. My son and I have taken the German, von Kalmbach. As he left the wall, dazed with fighting, we followed, guiding him subtly to the ruined tower whereof you know, and giving him drugged wine, bound him fast. Let my lord send the emir Mikhal Oglu to the wall by the tower, and we will give him into thy hands. We will bind him on the old mangonel and cast him over the wall like a tree trunk."

The Armenian took up an arrow and began to bind the parchment about the shaft with light silver wire.

"Take this to the roof, and shoot it toward the mantlet, as usual," he began, when Rhupen exclaimed, "Hark!" and both froze, their eyes glittering like those of trapped vermin—fearful yet vindictive.

Gottfried gnawed at the gag; it slipped. Outside he heard a familiar voice. "Gottfried! Where the devil are you?"

His breath burst from him in a stentorian roar. "Hey, Sonya! Name of the devil! Be careful, girl—"

Tshoruk snarled like a wolf and struck him savagely on the head with a scimitar hilt. Almost instantly, it seemed, the door crashed inward. As in a dream Gottfried saw Red Sonya framed in the doorway, pistol in hand. Her face was drawn and haggard; her eyes burned like coals. Her basinet was gone, and her scarlet cloak. Her mail was hacked and red-clotted, her boots slashed, her silken breeches splashed and spotted with blood.

With a croaking cry Tshoruk ran at her, scimitar lifted. Before he could strike, she crashed down the barrel of the empty pistol on his head, felling him like an ox. From the other side Rhupen slashed at her with a curved Turkish dagger. Dropping the pistol, she closed with the young Oriental. Moving like someone in a dream, she bore him irresistibly backward, one hand gripping his wrist, the other his throat. Throttling him slowly, she inexorably crashed his head again and again against the stones of the wall, until his eyes rolled up and set. Then she threw him from her like a sack of loose salt.

"God!" she muttered thickly, reeling an instant in the center of the room, her hands to her head. Then she went to the captive and sinking stiffly to her knees, cut his bonds with fumbling strokes that sliced his flesh as well as the cords.

"How did you find me?" he asked stupidly, clambering stiffly up.

She reeled to the table and sank down in a chair. A flagon of wine stood at her elbow and she seized it avidly and drank. Then she wiped her mouth on her sleeve and surveyed him wearily but with renewed life.

"I saw you leave the wall and followed. I was so drunk from the fighting I scarce knew what I did. I saw those dogs take your arm and lead you into the alleys, and then I lost sight of you. But I found your burganet lying outside in the street, and began shouting for you. What the hell's the meaning of this?"

She picked up the arrow, and blinked at the parchment fastened to it. Evidently she could read the Turkish characters, but she scanned it half a dozen times before the meaning became apparent to her exhaustion-numbed brain. Then her eyes flickered dangerously to the men on the floor. Tshoruk sat up, dazedly feeling the gash in his scalp; Rhupen lay retching and gurgling on the floor.

"Tie them up, brother," she ordered, and Gottfried obeyed. The victims eyed the woman much more apprehensively than him.

"This missive is addressed to Ibrahim, the Wezir," she said abruptly. "Why does he want Gottfried's head?"

"Because of a wound he gave the Sultan at Mohacz," muttered Tshoruk uneasily.
"And you, you lower-than-a-dog," she smiled mirthlessly, "you fired the mine by the Karnthner! You and your spawn are the traitors among us."
She drew and primed a pistol. "When Zrinyi learns of you," she said, "your end will be neither quick nor sweet. But first, you old swine, I'm going to give myself the pleasure of blowing out your cub's brains before your eyes—"
The older Armenian gave a choking cry. "God of my fathers, have mercy! Kill me—torture me—but spare my son!"
At that instant a new sound split the unnatural quiet—a great peal of bells shattered the air.
"What's this?" roared Gottfried, groping wildly at his empty scabbard.
"The bells of Saint Stephen!" cried Sonya. "They peal for victory!"

She sprang for the sagging stair and he followed her up the perilous way. They came out on a sagging shattered roof, on a firmer part of which stood an ancient stone-casting machine, relic of an earlier age, and evidently recently repaired.
The tower overlooked an angle of the wall, at which there were no watchers. A section of the ancient glacis, and a ditch interior the main moat, coupled with a steep natural pitch of the earth beyond, made the point practically invulnerable.
The spies had been able to exchange messages here with little fear of discovery, and it was easy to guess the method used. Down the slope, just within long arrow-shot, stood up a huge mantlet of bullhide stretched on a wooden frame, as if abandoned there by chance. Gottfried knew that message-laden arrows were loosed from the tower roof into this mantlet.
But just then he gave little thought to that. His attention was riveted on the Turkish camp. There a leaping glare paled the spreading dawn; above the mad clangor of the bells rose the crackle of flames, mingled with awful screams.
"The Janizaries are burning their prisoners," said Red Sonya.
"Judgment Day in the morning," muttered Gottfried, awed at the sight that met his eyes.
From their eyrie the companions could see almost all of the plain. Under a cold gray leaden sky, tinged a somber crimson with dawn, it lay strewn with Turkish corpses as far as the sight would carry.

And the hosts of the living were melting away. From Semmering the great pavilion had vanished. The other tents were now coming down fast. Already the head of the long column was out of sight, moving into the hills through the cold dawn.

Snow began falling in light swift flakes.

"They shot their bolt last night," said Red Sonya to von Kalmbach. "I saw their officers lashing them, and heard them cry out in fear beneath our swords. Flesh and blood could stand no more.

The snow continued to fall.

The Janizaries were glutting their mad disappointment on their helpless captives, hurling men, women and children living into the flames they had kindled under the somber eyes of their master, the monarch men called the Magnificent, the Merciful. All the time the bells of Vienna clanged and thundered as if their bronze throats would burst.

Look!" cried Red Sonya, and she clutched her companion's arm. "The Akinji will form the rear-guard."

Even at that distance they made out a pair of vulture wings moving among the dark masses; the sullen light glimmered on a jeweled helmet. Sonya's powder-stained hands clenched so that the pink, broken nails bit into the white palms, and she spat out a Cossack curse that burned like vitriol.

"There he goes, the bastard that made Austria a desert! How easily the souls of the butchered folk ride on his cursed winged shoulders! Anyway, old warhorse, he didn't get your head."

"While he lives it'll ride loose on my shoulders," rumbled the giant.

Red Sonya's keen eyes narrowed suddenly. Seizing Gottfried's arm, she hurried downstairs. They did not see Nikolas Zrinyi and Paul Bakics ride out of the gates with their tattered retainers, risking their lives in sorties to rescue prisoners. Steel clashed along the line of march, and the Akinji retreated slowly, fighting a good rear-guard action, balking the headlong courage of the attackers by their very numbers. Safe in the depths of his horsemen, Mikhal Oglu grinned sardonically. But Suleyman, riding in the main column, did not grin. His face was like a death-mask.

Back in the ruined tower, Red Sonya propped one booted foot on a chair, and cupping her chin in her hand, stared into the fear-dulled eyes of Tshoruk.

"What will you give for your life?"

The Armenian made no reply.

"What will you give for the life of your whelp?"
The Armenian started as if stung. "Spare my son, princess," he groaned. "Anything—I will pay—I will do anything."
She threw a shapely booted leg across the chair and sat down.
"I want you to bear a message to a man."
"What man?"
"Mikhal Oglu."
He shuddered and moistened his lips with his tongue.
"Instruct me; I obey," he whispered.
"Good. We'll free you and give you a horse. Your son shall remain here as hostage. If you fail us, I'll give the cub to the Viennese to play with—"
Again the old Armenian shuddered.
"But if you play squarely, we'll let you both go free, and my pal and I will forget about this treachery. I want you to ride after Mikhal Oglu and tell him—"

Through the slush and driving snow, the Turkish column plodded slowly. Horses bent their heads to the blast; up and down the straggling lines camels groaned and complained, and oxen bellowed pitifully. Men stumbled through the mud, leaning beneath the weight of their arms and equipment. Night was falling, but no command had been given to halt. All day the retreating host had been harried by the daring Austrian cuirassiers who darted down upon them like wasps, tearing captives from their very hands.
Grimly rode Suleyman among his Solaks. He wished to put as much distance as possible between himself and the scene of his first defeat, where the rotting bodies of thirty thousand Muhammadans reminded him of his crushed ambitions. Lord of western Asia he was; master of Europe he could never be. Those despised walls had saved the Western world from Moslem dominion, and Suleyman knew it. The rolling thunder of the Ottoman power re-echoed around the world, paling the glories of Persia and Mogul India. But in the West the yellow-haired Aryan barbarian stood unshaken. It was not written that the Turk should rule beyond the Danube.
Suleyman had seen this written in blood and fire, as he stood on Semmering and saw his warriors fall back from the ramparts, despite the flailing lashes of their officers. It had been to save his authority that he gave the order to break camp—it burned his tongue like gall, but already his soldiers were burning their tents and preparing to

desert him. Now in darkly brooding silence he rode, not even speaking to Ibrahim.

In his own way Mikhal Oglu shared their savage despondency. It was with a ferocious reluctance that he turned his back on the land he had ruined, as a half-glutted panther might be driven from its prey. He recalled with satisfaction the blackened, corpse-littered wastes—the screams of tortured men—the cries of girls writhing in his iron arms; recalled with much the same sensations the death-shrieks of those same girls in the blood-fouled hands of his killers.

But he was stung with the disappointment of a task undone—for which the Grand Vizier had lashed him with stinging word. He was out of favor with Ibrahim. For a lesser man that might have meant a bowstring. For him it meant that he would have to perform some prodigious feat to reinstate himself. In this mood he was dangerous and reckless as a wounded panther.

Snow fell heavily, adding to the miseries of the retreat. Wounded men fell in the mire and lay still, covered by a growing white mantle. Mikhal Oglu rode among his rearmost ranks, straining his eyes into the darkness. No foe had been sighted for hours. The victorious Austrians had ridden back to their city.

The columns were moving slowly through a ruined village, whose charred beams and crumbling fire-seared walls stood blackly in the falling snow. Word came back down the lines that the Sultan would pass on through and camp in a valley which lay a few miles beyond. The quick drum of hoofs back along the way they had come caused the Akinji to grip their lances and glare slit-eyed into the flickering darkness. They heard but a single horse, and a voice calling the name of Mikhal Oglu. With a word the chief stayed a dozen lifted bows, and shouted in return. A tall, gray stallion loomed out of the flying snow, a black-mantled figure crouched grotesquely atop of it.

"Tshoruk! You Armenian dog! What in the name of Allah—"

The Armenian rode close to Mikhal Oglu and whispered urgently in his ear. The cold bit through the thickest garments. The Akinji noted that Tshoruk was trembling violently. His teeth chattered and he stammered in his speech. But the Turk's eyes blazed at the import of his message.

"Dog, do you lie?"

"May I rot in hell if I lie!" A strong shudder shook Tshoruk and he drew his kaftan close about him. "He fell from his horse, riding with the cuirassiers to attack the rear-guard, and lies with a broken leg in a deserted peasant's hut some three miles back—alone except for his mistress Red Sonya, and three or four Lanzknechts, who are drunk on wine they found in the deserted camp."

Mikhal Oglu wheeled his horse with sudden intent.

"Twenty men to me!" he barked. "The rest ride on with the main column. I go after a head worth its weight in gold. I'll overtake you before you go in camp."

Othman caught his jeweled rein. "Are you mad, to ride back now? The whole country will be on our heels—"

He reeled in his saddle as Mikhal Oglu slashed him across the mouth with his riding whip. The chief wheeled away, followed by the men he had designated. Like ghosts they vanished into the spectral darkness. Othman sat his horse uncertainly, looking after them. The snow shafted down, the wind sobbed drearily among the bare branches. There was no sound except the receding noises of the trudging column. Presently these ceased. Then Othman started. Back along the way they had come, he heard a distant reverberation, a roar as of forty or fifty matchlocks speaking together. In the utter silence which followed, panic came upon Othman and his warriors. Whirling away they fled through the ruined village after the retreating horde.

CHAPTER 7

NONE NOTICED when night fell on Constantinople, for the splendor of Suleyman made night no less glorious than day. Through gardens that were riots of blossoms and perfume, cressets twinkled like myriad fireflies. Fireworks turned the city into a realm of shimmering magic, above which the minarets of five hundred mosques rose like towers of fire in an ocean of golden foam. Tribesmen on Asian hills gaped and marveled at the blaze that pulsed and glowed afar, paling the very stars. The streets of Stamboul were thronged with crowds in the attire of holiday and rejoicing. The million lights shone on jeweled turban and striped khalat—on dark eyes sparkling over filmy veils—on shining palanquins borne on the shoulders of huge ebony-skinned slaves.

All that splendor centered in the Hippodrome, where in lavish pageants the horsemen of Turkistan and Tatary competed in breathtaking races with the riders of Egypt and Arabia, where warriors in glittering mail spilled one another's blood on the sands, where swordsmen were matched against wild beasts, and lions were pitted against tigers of Bengal and boars from northern forests. One might have deemed the imperial pageantry of Rome revived in Eastern garb. On a golden throne, set upon lapis lazuli pillars, Suleyman reclined, gazing on the splendors, as purple-togaed Caesars had gazed before him. About him bowed his viziers and officers, and the ambassadors from foreign courts—Venice, Persia, India, the khanates of Tatary. They came—including the Venetians—to congratulate him on his victory over the Austrians. For this grand fete was in celebration of that victory, as set forth in a manifesto under the Sultan's hand, which stated, in part, that the Austrians having made submission and sued for pardon on their knees, and the German realms being so distant from the Ottoman empire, "the Faithful would not trouble to clean out the fortress (Vienna), or purify, improve, and put it in repair." Therefore the Sultan had accepted the submission of the contemptible Germans, and left them in possession of their paltry "fortress"!

Suleyman was blinding the eyes of the world with the blaze of his wealth and glory, and striving to make himself believe that he had actually accomplished all he had intended. He had not been beaten on the field of open battle; he had set his puppet on the Hungarian throne; he had devastated Austria; the markets of Stamboul and Asia were full of Christian slaves. With this knowledge he soothed his vanity, ignoring the fact that thirty thousand of his subjects rotted before Vienna, and that his dreams of European conquest had been shattered.

Behind the throne shone the spoils of war—silken and velvet pavilions, wrested from the Persians, the Arabs, the Egyptian memluks; costly tapestries, heavy with gold embroidery. At his feet were heaped the gifts and tributes of subject and allied princes. There were vests of Venetian velvet, golden goblets crusted with jewels from the courts of the Grand Moghul, ermine-lined kaftans from Erzeroum, carven jade from Cathay, silver Persian helmets with horse-hair plumes, turban-cloths, cunningly sewn with gems, from Egypt, curved Damascus blades of watered steel, matchlocks from Kabul worked richly in chased silver, breastplates and shields of Indian steel, rare furs from Mongolia.

The throne was flanked on either hand by a long rank of youthful slaves, made fast by golden collars to a single, long silver chain. One file was composed of young Greek and Hungarian boys, the other of girls; all clad only in plumed head-pieces and jeweled ornaments intended to emphasize their nudity.

Eunuchs in flowing robes, their rotund bellies banded by cloth-of-gold sashes, knelt and offered the royal guests sherbets in gemmed goblets, cooled with snow from the mountains of Asia Minor. The torches danced and flickered to the roars of the multitudes. Around the courses swept the horses, foam flying from their bits; wooden castles reeled and went up in flames as the Janizaries clashed in mock warfare. Officers passed among the shouting people, tossing showers of copper and silver coins amongst them. None hungered or thirsted in Stamboul that night except the miserable Caphar captives.

The minds of the foreign envoys were numbed by the bursting sea of splendor, the thunder of imperial magnificence. About the vast arena stalked trained elephants, almost covered with housings of gold-worked leather, and from the jeweled towers on their backs, fanfares of trumpets vied with the roar of the throngs and the bellowing of lions. The tiers of the Hippodrome were a sea of faces, all turning toward the jeweled figure on the shining throne, while thousands of tongues wildly thundered his acclaim.

As he impressed the Venetian envoys, Suleyman knew he impressed the world. In the blaze of his magnificence, men would forget that a handful of desperate Caphars behind rotting walls had closed his road to empire. Suleyman accepted a goblet of the forbidden wine, and spoke aside to the Grand Vizier, who stepped forth and lifted his arms.

"Oh, guests of my master, the Padishah forgets not the humblest in the hour of rejoicing. To the officers who led his hosts against the infidels, he has made rare gifts. Now he gives two hundred and forty thousand ducats to be distributed among the common soldiers, and likewise to each Janizary he gives a thousand aspers."

In the midst of the roar that went up, a eunuch knelt before the Grand Vizier, holding up a large round package, carefully bound and sealed. A folded piece of parchment, held shut by a red seal, accompanied it. The attention of the Sultan was attracted.

"Oh, friend, what has thou there?"

Ibrahim salaamed. "The rider of the Adrianople post delivered it, oh Lion of Islam. Apparently it is a gift of some sort from the Austrian dogs. Infidel riders, I understand, gave it into the hands of the border guard, with instructions to send it straightway to Stamboul."

"Open it," directed Suleyman, his interest roused. The eunuch salaamed to the floor, then began breaking the seals of the package. A scholarly slave opened the accompanying note and read the contents,

written in a bold yet feminine hand:
To the Soldan Suleyman and his Wezir Ibrahim and to the hussy Roxelana we who sign our names below send a gift in token of our immeasurable fondness and kind affection.

Sonya of Rogatino, and Gottfried von Kalmbach
Suleyman, who had started up at the name of his favorite, his features suddenly darkening with wrath, gave a choking cry, which was echoed by Ibrahim.
The eunuch had torn the seals of the bale, disclosing what lay within. A pungent scent of herbs and preservative spices filled the air, and the object, slipping from the horrified eunuch's hands, tumbled among the heaps of presents at Suleyman's feet, offering a ghastly contrast to the gems, gold and velvet bales. The Sultan stared down at it and in that instant his shimmering pretense of triumph slipped from him; his glory turned to tinsel and dust. Ibrahim tore at his beard with a gurgling, strangling sound, purple with rage.
At the Sultan's feet, the features frozen in a death-mask of horror, lay the severed head of Mikhal Oglu, Vulture of the Grand Turk.

FROM PUBLIC DOMAIN SUPER HEROES BY THE SAME AUTHOR

HOUSE OF JUSTICE

Captain Midnight™ And The Sizzling Spider In: Dr. Satan And The Element Of Evil

Say The Magic Word! Captain Marvel Begins! (February 2026)

HOUSE OF CROM™

Swords In The House Of Horus: A Lost Scroll Of Kull Of Atlantis™

Bran Mak Morn™ And The Amazons Of Atlantis (January 2026)

HOUSE OF DREAD

Red SonYa™ Of Rogatino: The Shadow Of Tanaghaara

Day Ripper (March 2026)

HOUSE OF ENTROPY

The Metropolis Of Mongo™: Buck Rogers And Wilma Deering. Out of Time.

The Marine Moon Of Mongo™: Crash Corrigan In The Undersea Kingdom (April 2026)

)

HOUSE OF GREYBISHOP

Quarks & Re-Creation

The Ease Of Taking (December 2025)

Bred In The Bone *Morgan's Lament Book 1*

Bones Of Contention *Morgan's Lament Book 2*

Skein And Bones *Morgan's Lament Book 3* (Summer/Fall 2026)

Printed in Dunstable, United Kingdom

84199594R00109